📖 Title Page

The Lies We Weave

One lie. Countless consequences.

A Novel

by

Raven Dee

Published by **Self-Published**

2025

📜 Copyright Page

This is a work of fiction. Names, characters, businesses, places, events, and incidents are either products of the author's imagination or used fictitiously. Any resemblance to actual persons, living or dead, or real events is purely coincidental.

ISBN: 978-93-342-3242-4

Cover Design by: Raven Dee

Published by: Self- Published

Website: https://lotussutrabooks.com

Printed in India

Table of Contents

Dedication

To the dreamers, the seekers, and the ones who dare to venture into the unknown.

For those who believe in the balance of light and dark, in the power of transformation, and in the infinite possibilities of the universe.

This book is for you.

Acknowledgment

Writing this book has been a journey of discovery, challenges, and inspiration. I would like to express my deepest gratitude to:

- **My family and friends**, for their endless support and encouragement.
- **The mentors and guides**, who have shaped my understanding of storytelling and balance.
- **The readers**, whose curiosity and passion bring these words to life.
- **The unseen forces of creativity and intuition**, for guiding me through the depths of this story.

This book exists because of all of you. Thank you for being part of this journey.

Prologue: The Threads of Fate

The cosmos pulsed with a rhythm older than time itself. Between the worlds, where light and darkness met, the Void whispered secrets to those who dared to listen.

Kritika had always felt the presence of something beyond the visible realms. She had seen the fractures in reality, the silent wars between forces too great for most to comprehend. But the prophecy spoke of a time when the balance would shift—when the universe itself would demand a reckoning.

And that time had come.

The Ancient One stirred. The Void called to her.

The fate of the realms was about to be rewritten.

Chapter 1: Kritika – The Girl Who Loved Too Much

A Heart Full of Dreams

The scent of **freshly printed notebooks and sharpened pencils** filled the small room as **Kritika flipped through her old diary**. Each page was filled with lyrics from **90s Bollywood songs**, half-written love letters to a boy who didn't exist, and **sketches of nameless faces**—portraits of someone she wished would step into her life.

She sighed, **tapping her pen against the paper**, lost in thought.

Kritika had always been **a dreamer**. Not the kind who simply fantasized but one who **believed in the magic of love, in grand romantic gestures, in the way old Bollywood movies painted love—pure, passionate, and everlasting**.

But reality? Reality was nothing like the movies.

At **sixteen**, Kritika had never had a boyfriend. In a world where her classmates **giggled over text messages, showed off Valentine's Day gifts, and whispered secrets about stolen kisses**, she felt like **an outsider**.

She wasn't ugly. No, Kritika knew she had **kind eyes, soft features, and a smile that could light up a dull afternoon**. But she was **quiet, reserved**, more interested in writing poetry in the margins of her schoolbooks than discussing boys over lunch.

And that made her **invisible**.

A Family That Loved, But Didn't Understand

Her mother's voice broke her thoughts.

"Kritika! Stop daydreaming and help me in the kitchen!"

Sighing, she shut her diary and headed toward the tiny but cozy kitchen, where her mother was stirring tea in a **steel saucepan**. The aroma of **cardamom and ginger** filled the air.

"You need to stop wasting time writing those silly love stories," her mother scolded playfully, handing her a cup.

Kritika smiled, taking a sip. **Her mother never understood her fascination with love.** To her, love was **practical—a duty, a responsibility**. But for Kritika, love was **everything.**

Her father, a **quiet, hardworking man**, only nodded at her from behind his newspaper, while her **maternal grandparents adored her unconditionally**. It was a simple household, filled with routine and warmth, yet something inside her always craved more.

The Loneliness of School Hallways

School was supposed to be **a place of friendships, laughter, and unforgettable moments**.

For Kritika, it was just another place where she felt **like she didn't belong**.

As she walked through the hallway, she saw groups of girls huddled together, **giggling over something on a phone screen. She wanted to be part of that.** She wanted to sit in a circle and laugh over silly love stories, to have someone to share secrets with.

But instead, she was always on the **outside, looking in**.
Her classmates never **bullied** her, but they never truly **saw** her either.

The Lie That Started Everything

It started with a **simple question**.
That day, during lunch, Kritika sat with **Moni, Priya, and Neha**, the only girls she spoke to occasionally.
Moni, the **queen bee** of the group, leaned forward, her eyes gleaming with mischief. **"So, Kritika... do you have a boyfriend?"**
Kritika's **heart pounded**. The truth was a simple 'No.' But **her mind screamed at her not to say it**.
She saw the way Priya and Neha **smiled knowingly**, expecting the usual **shy shake of her head**.
But before she could stop herself, she **lied.**
"Yes."
The word felt **strange on her tongue**, but the moment it was out, it was too late to take it back.
Moni's eyes **widened in surprise**, while Priya and Neha **exchanged glances**.
"Really?" Moni smirked. "Tell us about him."
Kritika swallowed hard. She could feel her heart hammering in her chest. **What had she done?**
But as she looked into their curious, impressed eyes, she realized something.
For the first time, she **wasn't invisible**.
For the first time, she **was interesting**.

And that's when she knew—**this lie was just the beginning.**

Chapter 2: The Birth of a Dream Boyfriend

A Web of Lies Begins

Kritika's heartbeat **pounded in her ears** as Moni, Priya, and Neha waited eagerly for her to describe the **boyfriend that didn't exist**.

Moni, the sharpest of them all, **narrowed her eyes with curiosity**. **"So? Tell us! What's his name?"**

Kritika's mind **raced**. A name… she needed a name!

"Aarav." The name slipped from her lips before she could think twice. It sounded **perfect—romantic, mysterious, and slightly poetic.**

Priya gasped. "Ooooh! Aarav? That's such a dreamy name."

Neha, who usually stayed quiet, raised an eyebrow. **"And where did you meet him?"**

Kritika took a deep breath. If she was going to **build this lie, she needed to make it foolproof.**

"I met him at a wedding," she said confidently, surprising even herself.

Moni's face lit up with excitement. **"Whose wedding?"**

Crap.

She had spoken too quickly. But now there was no turning back.

"My cousin's wedding."

"Oh, that's so filmy!" Priya sighed dreamily. "Did he flirt with you first?"

"Of course," Kritika smiled, now gaining confidence. "He couldn't stop looking at me. And then he requested the DJ to play a song just for me."

The girls **gasped in unison**.

Moni leaned in, **intrigued**. **"Which song?"**

Kritika, a 90s song lover, instinctively said, **"Pehla Nasha."**

It was the **perfect answer**. A song about **first love, innocence, and dreamy romance**.

Priya placed a hand over her heart. **"Wow. That's straight out of a movie."**

Neha nodded, looking impressed. **"You've been hiding a love story like this from us all this time?"**

Kritika only **smiled, pretending to be shy**, but inside, she was **panicking**.

This wasn't just a small lie anymore. **This was a story. A whole relationship she now had to build, maintain, and protect.**

The Details That Made It Real

For the next few days, Kritika became **an actress in her own love story**.

Every morning at school, her friends **bombarded her with questions**.

- **"What does Aarav do?"**
- **"What's his favorite food?"**
- **"How do you both talk if he doesn't study in our school?"**

Kritika's mind worked fast.

She made Aarav **a college student—three years older than her**, mature but romantic. He loved **chai over coffee, blue over black, and old songs over new ones.** He was a **perfect gentleman**, always sending her **long goodnight texts**, always dedicating **90s songs to her**.

And as she spoke about him, something strange happened.

For a moment, even she started to believe he was real.

The Problem with Lies

One day, Moni came up to her with an **excited grin**.

"I have the best idea ever!" she announced.

Kritika frowned. **"What?"**

Moni pulled out her phone. **"Let's call Aarav! I want to talk to him."**

Kritika's **stomach dropped.**

Priya and Neha **perked up immediately**.

"Oh my God, yes! We should totally talk to him," Priya squealed.

Neha, the most serious of them all, nodded. **"Yeah, Kritika. We've never even seen a photo of him. Let's hear his voice at least."**

Panic **flooded Kritika's veins.**

What was she supposed to do now?

She had no boyfriend. No number. No Aarav.

But she couldn't back out now.

So she did what she had been doing all this time.

She lied again.

"I... I don't have a phone."

Moni raised an eyebrow. **"Really?"**

"Yeah," Kritika said quickly. **"My parents don't allow me to have one."**

Priya pouted. **"That's so unfair. So how do you talk to him?"**

Kritika swallowed. **"Um… on my cousin's phone. But only sometimes."**

Moni **studied her carefully**, as if trying to catch her in a lie. But before she could say anything, Priya sighed dramatically.

"That's so romantic. Old-school love."

The conversation **shifted**, and Kritika **exhaled in relief**.

But deep down, she knew.

This wasn't the end. It was just the beginning of a much bigger problem.

Chapter 3: Trapped in the Web of Lies

A Friend Turned Detective

Moni **wasn't convinced**.

Something about Kritika's story **felt off**—the way she avoided details, how she never had a phone, how she never showed any proof of Aarav's existence.

She had been friends with Kritika long enough to **see through her nervous smiles and hesitant answers**.

And Moni was not the kind of person to **let a mystery go unsolved**.

"I need to know the truth," she thought to herself.

That day, as soon as school ended, she **pulled Priya and Neha aside**.

"Guys," Moni said, lowering her voice. **"I think Kritika is lying about Aarav."**

Priya **gasped. "No way! She wouldn't lie about something like that."**

Neha, always the logical one, folded her arms. **"What makes you say that?"**

Moni smirked. **"Think about it. She has no phone. No photos. No texts. And whenever we ask to talk to him, she always has an excuse."**

Priya hesitated. **"But she seems so happy when she talks about him..."**

"Exactly," Moni said. **"Too happy. Like she's making up a dream boyfriend."**

Neha frowned. **"So what do you want to do?"**

Moni's eyes **gleamed with mischief**. **"Simple. We trap her in her own lie."**

The Setup

The next day, the three friends **waited for the perfect moment**.

During lunch break, when they were sitting together, Moni suddenly **let out an excited scream**.

"Kritika! Guess what?"

Kritika, who had been lost in her thoughts, **jumped in surprise**. **"What happened?"**

Moni grinned. **"I found Aarav on Facebook!"**

Kritika's **blood ran cold.**

What?! How?!

She had **never** created a fake account for Aarav.

How could Moni have found him?

"W-what do you mean?" Kritika stammered, trying to act normal.

Moni **giggled**. **"I just searched for Aarav with the details you gave us, and guess what? I found someone who matches exactly what you described! He even listens to 90s songs. I sent him a friend request."**

Priya and Neha **leaned in, excited**.

"No way! Kritika, you have to check!" Priya said, pulling out her phone.

Kritika's hands **felt ice cold**.

She knew there was no Aarav.

Moni was bluffing.

Testing her.

And now, if she panicked, it would **confirm her lie.**

The Escape Plan

Kritika **forced herself to laugh. "Oh, really? That's funny because my Aarav isn't on social media."**

Moni's **eyes narrowed.**

Neha and Priya exchanged glances.

"He isn't?" Neha asked.

"Nope," Kritika said quickly. **"He doesn't like social media. Too many distractions, he says."**

Moni smiled. But it wasn't a friendly smile.

It was the smile of someone who **knew she had just caught a liar.**

"That's interesting," Moni said slowly. **"Because I was actually bluffing. I never found anyone."**

The world **stopped**.

Kritika's stomach **dropped.**

Priya and Neha **looked at her, confused**.

And that's when Kritika knew.

She was caught.

The Aftermath

The air around them was **thick with tension**.

Kritika **felt her hands tremble** under the table. She needed to say something. **Anything.**

So she did **the only thing she could do.**

She **doubled down on her lie.**

"You think I'm lying?" she said, faking offense. **"That's really hurtful, Moni."**

Moni **didn't buy it.**

"Then prove it," she challenged. **"Let us talk to him. Just once."**

Priya and Neha **nodded**.

Kritika **felt trapped**.

She knew she couldn't keep lying forever. But she also couldn't tell the truth.

So she made a **desperate move.**

"I… I broke up with him," she blurted out.

Silence.

Moni, Priya, and Neha **stared at her.**

"What?" Priya whispered.

"Yeah," Kritika nodded, pretending to look sad. **"Last night. It was a long-distance relationship, and it wasn't working out."**

Priya **covered her mouth in shock. "Oh my God, Kritika! Why didn't you tell us?"**

Moni just watched her. Silent. Unmoving.

Kritika held her breath.

Had she fooled them?

After a long pause, Moni **finally spoke**.

"Hmm. That's… sad."

But the way she said it sent **shivers down Kritika's spine.**

Because Moni's face said something else.

She didn't believe her. Not one bit.

Chapter 4: A Lie Too Deep to Escape

A Dangerous Game Begins

Kritika thought she had **escaped** Moni's trap with her fake breakup story.

But Moni **wasn't the kind of person to let things go.**

For the next few days, she watched Kritika closely—**too closely.**

Every time they talked about relationships, Moni would **casually slip in a question** about Aarav.

"So, did Aarav try to call you after the breakup?"

"Did you guys at least stay friends?"

"He must have been heartbroken, right?"

Every question felt like a **knife pressing deeper into Kritika's guilt.**

And with each answer, she had to **lie even more.**

But the worst part?

She wasn't just **lying to them anymore.**

She was **starting to believe her own story.**

The New Boy in School

Then, something happened that **Kritika never saw coming.**

A **new boy** joined their school.

His name was **Raghav.**

Tall. Sharp features. A quiet confidence in his walk.

And the moment he entered their class, **Moni's eyes lit up with mischief.**

"Kritika," she whispered, nudging her. **"He looks like the kind of guy who'd be your type."**

Kritika **rolled her eyes. "Shut up, Moni."**

"No, seriously." Moni smirked. **"Maybe he can be your 'new' Aarav."**

Kritika's **heart stopped.**

Was Moni still testing her?

Or was she just **teasing her?**

Either way, Kritika **felt trapped.**

So she did the only thing she could—**she ignored Moni.**

But Moni wasn't done.

The next day, she did something unexpected.

She **introduced Raghav to Kritika.**

"Hey, Raghav," Moni said loudly, making sure everyone heard. **"Meet Kritika. She just got out of a serious relationship."**

Kritika **froze.**

Raghav raised an eyebrow. **"Oh? That's... interesting."**

Moni **grinned. "She likes old-school romance. 90s songs. All that dreamy love story stuff."**

Raghav smirked.

"Good to know."

And just like that...

A new problem entered Kritika's life.

The Whispering Shadows

Over the next few weeks, Kritika noticed something **strange.**

Raghav was **always around.**

He wasn't trying to befriend her.

He wasn't trying to flirt.

But **whenever she turned, he was there. Watching. Listening.**

And one day, she overheard something **that made her blood run cold.**

Two classmates were whispering near the school library.

"Did you hear? Moni thinks Kritika was lying about her boyfriend."

"Seriously? But she always seemed so happy talking about him."

"Yeah, well, Moni's sure something's off."

Kritika's **stomach twisted.**

Moni had started **spreading doubts about her.**

And now, **people were talking.**

A Silent Threat

That evening, as Kritika was packing her bag, she heard a **low voice behind her.**

"So, who's Aarav?"

She **spun around.**

It was Raghav.

Standing by the classroom door. Arms crossed. Eyes sharp.

Kritika's throat went dry. **"What?"**

Raghav took a step closer. **"Aarav. Your ex. Who was he?"**

Kritika **forced a smile. "Why do you care?"**

Raghav leaned in slightly. **"Because Moni doesn't believe he was real."**

Kritika's heartbeat **thundered in her ears.**

Raghav **tilted his head. "And honestly? I don't either."**

She was trapped.

Chapter 5: The Web of Lies Tightens

A Ticking Time Bomb

Kritika **felt the air leave her lungs.**

Raghav's eyes were locked onto hers, sharp and unyielding.

For a second, she considered telling the truth.

Maybe if she admitted it now, it wouldn't be that bad.

But then she thought about Moni.

About Neha and Priya.

About all the times they'd laughed together, believing her stories.

If they found out the truth now… it would all be over.

She couldn't let that happen.

So, she did what she had always done best.

She lied.

"Aarav?" She forced a chuckle. **"Why are you so interested in my past, Raghav?"**

Raghav didn't blink. **"Because something doesn't add up."**

Kritika **rolled her eyes, pretending to be annoyed.**

"He was real, okay? We broke up. End of story."

Raghav studied her for a moment.

Then, with a smirk, he leaned in and whispered, **"If he was real, then you won't mind proving it."**

Kritika's blood ran cold. **"What?"**

Raghav took a step back. **"Tell me one thing."**

She swallowed hard. **"What?"**

His smirk deepened. **"Where is Aarav now?"**

A Dangerous Bet

That night, Kritika tossed and turned in bed.

Raghav had planted **a dangerous seed.**

What if he didn't stop digging?

She needed a way to shut him up.

Fast.

The next day at school, Moni was waiting for her with a knowing grin.

"Raghav's been asking about Aarav."

Kritika's stomach twisted. **"Yeah, I know."**

Moni leaned in, her voice dangerously low. **"I hope you're not lying, Kritika."**

Kritika forced a laugh. **"Come on, Moni. Why would I lie about something like that?"**

Moni studied her, then shrugged. **"Alright. Then prove it."**

Kritika's pulse spiked. **"Prove it how?"**

Moni grinned. **"Show me his photo."**

Kritika's hands **turned ice cold.**

A Desperate Move

She had two choices.

1. **Admit the truth and lose everything.**
2. **Find a way to create Aarav.**

And there was **only one answer she could live with.**

She had to **make Aarav real.**

That night, Kritika **searched the internet for hours.**

She needed a photo—**someone who looked like the dreamy, old-school romantic guy she had described.**

Finally, she found one.

A random Instagram profile.

A guy she had never met.

Aarav was born.

The Big Reveal

The next day, Kritika walked into class, heart pounding.

Moni was waiting, arms crossed.

Kritika took a deep breath, pulled out her phone, and showed the picture.

Moni snatched the phone.

She stared at the screen for a long moment.

Then, she smirked. **"Hmm. Not bad."**

Kritika exhaled.

For now, she was safe.

But she had no idea **how dangerous the game had just become.**

Because now that Aarav was real…

Someone else was about to enter the story.

Chapter 6: The Truth Has Eyes

A Shiver Down the Spine

Kritika thought she had won.

She had Moni fooled.

She had the group's approval.

But what she didn't know… was that someone had already begun **pulling at the threads of her lie.**

Raghav.

And he was about to make a move that would send **chills down Kritika's spine.**

A Shadow Watching

Two days later, during the lunch break, Kritika was about to open her lunchbox when her phone buzzed.

A message.

From an unknown number.

Her stomach twisted as she read the words.

"So, this is your boyfriend, huh?"

Attached was the **same picture** of the fake Aarav she had shown Moni.

Kritika's fingers turned ice cold.

Her eyes darted around the cafeteria.

Who sent this?

Who knew?

Raghav.

He was watching her from across the room, arms folded, a smirk playing on his lips.
He lifted his phone, as if to say, **"Checkmate."**

The Trap Tightens

Kritika's pulse hammered. She knew she had to act fast.
But before she could respond, another message popped up.
"Let's play a game, Kritika. If you're telling the truth... let's see if Aarav texts you back."
Her heart dropped.
No. No. No.
Moni had never asked to see messages. But Raghav?
He was dangerous.
He was smart.
And he wasn't backing down.
Kritika forced herself to stay calm.
She typed back.
"Why are you so obsessed with my boyfriend?"
Raghav's smirk deepened as he read the message.
Then, he replied with just one word.
"Prove it."

A Desperate Gamble

Kritika had **two choices.**

1. **Admit she had been lying this whole time.**
2. **Take the biggest risk of her life.**

And Kritika never picked the easy road.

That night, she created a **fake account for Aarav.**

She used the same stolen Instagram picture.

She made a profile.

Aarav Verma.

She sent herself a message.

"Hey, love. Missing you."

Then, she waited.

She knew Raghav wouldn't stop until he saw a reply.

Tomorrow, she would show him.

Tomorrow, she would **win.**

But what she didn't know…

Was that tomorrow would change everything.

Because someone was about to message Aarav.

And it wasn't Kritika.

Chapter 7: The Real Face of the Lie

The Unexpected Message

The next day, Kritika sat in her usual spot in class, heart pounding.

It was time to show Raghav the proof.

She reached for her phone, checking her fake account.

A new message had arrived.

Kritika's breath caught in her throat as she read the text.

"Hi, Kritika. Is this your way of hiding behind someone else's face?"

Attached was another picture—the same photo she had stolen for **Aarav**—but this time, it had a watermark: **"Gagan Photography."**

Kritika felt the ground slip beneath her.

Gagan.

The boy Moni had been showing off as her 'real' boyfriend.

This was not supposed to happen.

Kritika quickly closed the phone and stuffed it into her bag.

Her fingers were shaking. **"How did Gagan find out?"**

Raghav's Stranglehold

Just as she was trying to process the message, she looked up and saw Raghav standing by the door, his gaze fixed on her with an unsettling intensity.

He didn't say a word, but the smirk on his face was enough.

He knew.

Kritika's breath caught. **How much does he know?**

Raghav leaned against the doorframe, watching her. **"Did you think I wouldn't find out?"**

Her thoughts scrambled for a response.

"I don't know what you're talking about."

But Raghav simply shook his head, taking a step closer. **"Your lies are too big to cover up, Kritika. And now, you've dragged someone else into it."**

Kritika felt the weight of his words.

It wasn't just about her anymore.

This was about Moni, too.

About everything she had worked to build.

Her entire world was about to unravel.

The Truth Behind the Camera

Raghav pulled out his phone, showing her a message thread.

"Gagan Photography."

There, in black and white, was a message from someone named **'Gagan Sharma'**—the same Gagan Moni had talked about, the one who Kritika had pretended was her 'Aarav.'

"Why are you using my photo without asking?"

Kritika froze.

The truth was staring her in the face.

The person behind the photo wasn't a random stranger; he was someone who **could destroy everything**.

And now, that very person had just stepped into her world.

A Life-Changing Choice

Kritika sat silently, her mind racing.

What was she going to do now?

Moni was out of the loop—she didn't know any of this was happening.

She had lied to everyone.

She had manipulated her friends into believing something that wasn't real.

The silence stretched on between her and Raghav. His eyes held a challenge, an unspoken promise that the game was far from over.

Kritika could feel the tension in the room, a force stronger than any of her lies.

She finally spoke, her voice barely above a whisper. **"What do you want, Raghav?"**

He smiled darkly, then stepped back. **"I want you to admit everything. No more games."**

Kritika swallowed hard, feeling trapped.

But then, just as she thought she might cave in, **an idea struck her.**

The Final Gamble

Kritika knew she couldn't let Raghav win.

She couldn't let him control her story.

So, she made a decision—a decision that would change everything.

She would take control of the narrative.

With her heart in her throat, she stood up and faced Raghav. **"I'll admit everything. But not here. Not now."**

Raghav raised an eyebrow. **"Oh? And where would you like to do that?"**

Kritika met his gaze with newfound confidence.

"After school. You and me. In front of everyone."

Raghav's smirk faltered. **"What are you planning?"**

Kritika turned and walked toward the door, her mind already racing ahead. **"We'll see who's telling the truth, Raghav. Once and for all."**

Chapter 8: The Ultimate Reveal

The Day of Reckoning

Kritika's heart raced as she sat in her room, staring at the clock.

It was almost time.

After the tension-filled confrontation with Raghav, there was no turning back. She had agreed to meet him after school, in front of everyone. The stakes had never been higher, and the truth would come out in full force.

Moni had no idea what was coming. The lies had spiraled too far, too fast. What had started as a harmless exaggeration had grown into a tangled web of deceit. And now, the moment of truth was finally upon her.

Kritika took a deep breath.

Her plan was risky. She had no idea how it would unfold, but there was no other choice. She needed to confront everything head-on. No more running away. No more hiding.

The Gathering Storm

As the bell rang, signaling the end of the school day, Kritika walked to the courtyard where Raghav had instructed her to meet. Her stomach churned with anxiety, but her resolve remained strong.

The group of friends—Moni, Priya, Neha—were already there, gathered in a tight circle. Moni stood in the center, looking confident as usual, chatting with the others. She hadn't yet noticed Kritika's arrival.

Kritika walked slowly toward them, her footsteps echoing in the silence that seemed to have enveloped her world. The air felt thick with anticipation. As soon as Moni saw her, a smile spread across her face.

"Kritika! What took you so long?"

Kritika smiled weakly. **"I had to talk to Raghav."**

Raghav, who had been leaning against the wall, suddenly straightened up. He nodded at Kritika, signaling that it was time.

Without hesitation, Kritika stood in the middle of the group. She could feel the weight of everyone's eyes on her, waiting for her to speak.

The Truth Comes Crashing Down

Kritika took a deep breath.

"I've lied. And I'm here to admit it."

Her voice was calm, but the words hit like a thunderclap. The group fell silent, eyes wide in shock. Moni's smile faltered for a brief moment, then returned, though it was no longer as confident.

"What do you mean?" Moni asked, her voice laced with confusion.

Kritika looked at her friends—Priya, Neha—and then at Raghav. She knew that the moment she spoke, there would be no turning back.

"I don't have a boyfriend," Kritika continued, **"I've never had one. I've been pretending this whole time."**

Moni's eyes widened. **"What?"** she gasped. **"But you—"**

"It was all a lie," Kritika interrupted. **"I made it up because I was afraid you wouldn't accept me if I didn't have a boyfriend like everyone else. I didn't know how to fit in. So I created a fantasy."**

The group stared at her in disbelief. Kritika's heart raced as she spoke, each word harder to say than the last. But she had to do this.

"I used fake pictures. I used someone else's identity. And I lied to you all. I'm sorry."

Moni's Betrayal

Moni stood frozen, shock written all over her face. She was the last person Kritika had expected to feel betrayed by, but the truth hit harder than she could have imagined.

Then, in a quiet voice, Moni asked, **"So... the pictures... of Gagan...?"**

Kritika nodded.

"It was all fake. I never even met him. The photo I used was from a photographer's website."

There was a long pause.

Then Moni's expression darkened. **"You lied to me. You lied to all of us. And you think that makes everything okay?"**

Kritika's stomach dropped. **"I never meant to hurt you."**

But Moni was too angry to listen. She turned to Raghav, her voice seething. **"You knew all along, didn't you?"**

Raghav didn't flinch. **"I found out the truth when Kritika's fake account was exposed. I knew it would all come crashing down eventually."**

Moni's eyes burned with fury. **"I can't believe you."**

Kritika flinched. **"I'm sorry. I never wanted any of this."**

But the damage was done. Moni's trust was shattered, and so was the fragile friendship they had built.

A Twisted Turn

Just as Kritika was about to apologize again, Priya spoke up. Her voice was calm but firm.

"Kritika, I get it. You were trying to fit in, but you didn't have to lie to us. We could have accepted you for who you are."

Neha added, **"We're your friends, Kritika. But you've hurt us. It's going to take time to rebuild what's been broken."**

Kritika's heart sank. She knew they were right. The damage was done. But she wasn't ready to give up.

Just then, the sound of a phone ringing broke the silence.

It was **Moni's phone**. She picked it up, glanced at the screen, and her face went pale.

"What is it?" Kritika asked, her curiosity piqued.

Moni looked at the phone, then back at Kritika with a mix of anger and disbelief.

"Gagan... he's calling me."

Kritika's eyes widened. She hadn't expected that.

But something about the way Moni looked at the phone sent a chill down her spine.

Was there more to Gagan than she had ever known?

Chapter 9: The Hidden Truth

The Unanswered Call

The ringing of Moni's phone echoed through the air, intensifying the tension between the group. Everyone stood frozen, eyes darting between Moni and Kritika, the atmosphere thick with unspoken questions.

Moni, still holding the phone, stared at the screen in disbelief. The name on the display made Kritika's heart skip a beat.

"Gagan," Moni whispered, her voice trembling. **"Why is he calling me now?"**

Kritika's breath caught in her throat. This was the moment she had feared—the moment when the lies she had created would take on a life of their own and consume everything in their path.

"Maybe you should answer it," Priya suggested cautiously, her voice filled with a mix of curiosity and concern.

Moni shook her head. **"I don't know. I..."**

But the call kept ringing. Moni hesitated for a moment, then, against her better judgment, swiped the screen to answer.

"Hello?" Moni's voice was low, almost apprehensive.

The others leaned in slightly, trying to catch a glimpse of Moni's reaction. There was a long pause on the other end of the line, before Gagan's voice finally came through. But it wasn't what they expected.

"Moni," Gagan's voice was urgent, filled with an odd tension. **"I need to talk to you. There's something I need to tell you... something important."**

Moni's face changed. The initial shock gave way to confusion, then fear. **"What is it? Is everything okay?"**

"We need to meet. Right now. It's about Kritika."

The words sent a chill down Kritika's spine. Her mind raced, trying to connect the dots. **What did Gagan want with her?** Why was he calling Moni now, after all this time?

A Sinister Revelation

Moni, still holding the phone, glanced nervously at Kritika. **"What does he mean? What's going on, Kritika?"**

Kritika's heart pounded as she struggled to find the right words. She had no idea what Gagan could be referring to. He was supposed to be a part of her lie—a mere figment of her imagination. But now, everything was spiraling out of control.

"I don't know," she whispered, her voice trembling. **"But whatever it is, we need to hear him out. Let's meet him."**

Raghav, who had been silently observing the conversation, stepped forward. **"This doesn't feel right. Something's off."**

Moni's eyes flickered between Kritika and Raghav. She was visibly shaken but still seemed torn between curiosity and suspicion.

"Are you sure we should go?" she asked, glancing at Kritika.

Kritika hesitated for a moment, but then nodded. **"We have no choice. We need to face this head-on."**

With a reluctant nod, Moni ended the call, and the group began to prepare for the meeting with Gagan. But as they gathered their things and left the courtyard, Kritika couldn't shake the nagging feeling that something far more sinister was lurking beneath the surface.

The Encounter

The meeting spot was an old, deserted park near the outskirts of the city—a place Kritika had never been before. The air was heavy with the smell of damp earth and the distant hum of traffic. The trees surrounding the park seemed to whisper in the wind, and the shadow of the setting sun cast long, eerie shapes across the ground.

As the group arrived, they saw a figure standing by the park's entrance. It was Gagan.

But the man standing before them was nothing like the image Kritika had fabricated in her mind. He was older, his face lined with years of experience, and his eyes—cold and calculating—did not match the warm, carefree boy she had imagined. His gaze seemed to pierce through her, as though he could see right into her soul.

"You're late," Gagan said, his voice smooth but edged with something darker.

Kritika swallowed hard. **"I—I'm sorry. We didn't know where to find you."**

Gagan's eyes flicked toward Moni. **"You brought her here,"** he said, his tone carrying an undertone of warning. **"Good. It's time for all of you to know the truth."**

Kritika's stomach churned. **"What do you mean?"** she asked, her voice barely a whisper.

Gagan stepped forward, his expression unreadable. **"The truth about the lies you've been living in, Kritika. And the truth about me."**

Unveiling the Past

Kritika stood frozen, unsure of what to expect. Gagan's words had an ominous weight to them, and the last thing she wanted was for her carefully constructed world to come crumbling down. But it seemed that was exactly what was happening.

"What are you talking about?" Moni asked, her voice sharp with confusion.

Gagan gave a dark chuckle. **"I knew about your little 'relationship,' Kritika. I was the one who planted the pictures. I was the one who manipulated you into thinking that you could keep the lie going forever."**

Moni looked at Gagan, then at Kritika. **"What is this? Why would you do that?"**

Kritika's mind spun. The pieces were starting to fall into place, but the picture wasn't one she had expected.

"You've been lying to everyone, Moni. To yourself," Gagan continued. **"I'm not the person you think I am. I'm**

not the boyfriend you've been pretending to have. And I'm certainly not someone who's going to let you off the hook so easily."

Kritika's eyes widened. **"What do you want from me?"**

Gagan's smile twisted. **"What I want from you, Kritika, is much more than you can imagine. And what you'll give me... will change everything."**

The Twist That No One Saw Coming

At that moment, something strange happened. Moni, who had been standing silently, suddenly stepped forward, her expression shifting from confusion to determination.

"This has gone too far," Moni said, her voice steady. **"Gagan, you've been manipulating everyone. But now it's time to end this."**

Gagan's eyes narrowed. **"You think you can stop me? You don't even know who I really am. You never did."**

Suddenly, the truth came crashing down—Gagan wasn't just some random guy from the fabricated world Kritika had built. He was connected to something much darker, something that neither she nor Moni could have ever anticipated.

To be continued...

💭 **What is Gagan really after? What is the truth that will change everything for Kritika, Moni, and their group of friends?** Stay tuned for the next chapter!

Chapter 10: The Secrets Unraveled

The Betrayal

The air around Kritika felt thick with the weight of the truth—something darker than she had ever imagined. Gagan's words echoed in her ears, but her mind refused to comprehend what they truly meant. She stood there, frozen, caught in the crossfire of lies that had spiraled far beyond her control.

Moni stepped forward, her posture rigid, a sense of determination behind her every move. **"Gagan, you've been playing us all. It ends now,"** she declared.

But Gagan just smiled. It wasn't a kind smile, but one that sent a chill down Kritika's spine. **"You think you can stop me? You've been a pawn in a much bigger game than you know."**

The realization hit Kritika like a bolt of lightning. This was no ordinary lie; this was something far more sinister. And she had unknowingly walked straight into the trap.

"A game?" Moni scoffed. **"What game, Gagan?"**

He stepped closer, his eyes gleaming with something cold and dangerous. **"You really don't know, do you? Everything you've believed about me, about the stories you've been telling... none of it was real. It was all orchestrated. The lies, the manipulation... all of it was to get you here, right now, so you could witness what's really happening."**

Kritika's heart raced, her breathing shallow. **"What are you talking about? Who are you?"**
Gagan leaned in, lowering his voice to a whisper that only the group could hear. **"I'm someone who's been watching you, Kritika. And I've been waiting for the perfect moment to reveal the truth."**

The Unlikely Revelation

The truth Gagan spoke wasn't just about him, or even about the fabricated world Kritika had built around herself. It was much deeper—an intricate web of manipulation, deceit, and secrets that had been hidden from everyone, especially from Kritika.
"You're part of something bigger than you think, Kritika," Gagan continued, his voice cold. **"You were never meant to be just a girl with a lie. You were chosen."**
Kritika stared at him, her mind struggling to piece together the puzzle. She had never seen herself as anything special. Just a girl from a middle-class family, trying to fit in, trying to live out her dreams of love. But Gagan's words cut through her self-doubt, exposing the reality she had never considered.
"Chosen?" Moni's voice cracked. **"Chosen for what? What is all this?"**
Gagan turned to Moni, his eyes narrowing. **"You've been chasing the wrong things, Moni. It's not about love or friends. It's about power."**

Kritika's heart skipped a beat. **"What do you mean, power?"**

"Your family," Gagan said, looking directly at Kritika. **"They've been keeping secrets from you. Secrets about your heritage, your past. You're not just any ordinary girl, Kritika. You come from a long line of people who have been guarding something—something powerful. And now, you've become a target."**

The Unspoken Truth

The pieces of the puzzle clicked into place, but the bigger question remained unanswered. **Why? Why her?**

"What are you talking about?" Kritika demanded, her voice shaky but strong. **"Why would anyone want me? What do you mean by 'guarding something'?"**

Gagan's expression hardened, his eyes flicking to Moni before returning to Kritika. **"You've always felt like you were different, haven't you? Like there was something more to your life than what you could see. The singing, the dancing, the dreams of a perfect love story—it's all part of something deeper."**

"Stop! Stop playing games!" Moni's voice cracked, but she couldn't hide her own growing fear.

Gagan's gaze softened slightly. **"It's not a game, Moni. It's your reality. It's all connected. The dreams, the lies, the betrayals—it's all part of the plan."**

Kritika's mind reeled. She had spent so much of her life wanting something simple: love, friendship, a place to belong. But this—this new reality—was a nightmare she had never asked for.

"I don't understand," Kritika whispered. **"What plan? What do you want from me?"**

Gagan sighed, his voice almost sympathetic. **"What I want isn't important. What matters is what you're going to do with this knowledge. Are you going to run, or are you going to fight?"**

The Decision

The weight of Gagan's words pressed heavily on Kritika's shoulders. Her heart raced with fear, but something else—a deep sense of determination—began to stir within her.

"What do you mean, fight?" she asked, her voice shaking but with a newfound strength.

Gagan's eyes glinted with something dark. **"You're more capable than you know. You just have to embrace it. The powers within you, the gifts you've been hiding from the world—they can help you fight back. But you'll need to choose. Choose to accept your past, your legacy, or let it all slip away."**

Kritika stood silent for a moment, her mind racing. She thought about everything she had been through—every lie, every twist and turn. She thought about her family, her friends, the love she had craved. But most of all, she thought about who she wanted to become.

This wasn't just about her anymore. This was about something bigger—something that was calling to her, whether she was ready or not.

"I'm not running," Kritika said, her voice steady. **"I won't let this define me. I'll fight. I'll find out the truth. And I'll make it right."**

Moni stepped forward, a look of determination in her eyes. **"We're with you, Kritika. No matter what happens, we're in this together."**

The Twist: An Unforeseen Ally

Just as the group was beginning to process Gagan's chilling words, a shadow moved from behind the trees. Out of the darkness stepped a figure—someone Kritika never expected to see.

It was Neha.

"I knew you'd find out eventually," Neha said, her voice calm but tinged with a strange seriousness. **"I've been waiting for you to come to your senses."**

Kritika's heart skipped. **"Neha? What are you doing here?"**

Neha's expression softened, but there was a hard edge to her gaze. **"I'm not who you think I am, Kritika. I'm not just the quiet girl in the background. I've known the truth all along."**

To be continued...

Chapter 11: Unveiling Hidden Truths

The Unexpected Ally

Kritika's heart pounded in her chest as Neha stepped into the light, her expression calm yet filled with something deeper—something darker. Kritika had always thought of Neha as the quiet one, the one who stayed out of the drama and observed from the sidelines. But now, standing in front of her, Neha looked like a completely different person.

"Neha," Kritika whispered, taking a step back. **"What do you mean you knew? What truth are you talking about?"**

Neha's gaze never faltered as she looked at Kritika. **"I've been watching, Kritika. Watching you struggle, trying to fit in with the lies. I knew one day you'd find out what's really going on."**

Moni, still standing beside Kritika, looked at Neha suspiciously. **"What do you know, Neha? Are you part of this too?"**

Neha shook her head slowly, her eyes never leaving Kritika's face. **"No, I'm not part of it. But I've known something you haven't. Something that's been hidden from all of you… especially from you, Kritika."**

Kritika's mind raced. **"What are you talking about?"** she asked, her voice growing more anxious with each passing second. **"What's been hidden from me?"**

Neha took a deep breath and spoke, her words carrying the weight of something that had been buried for a long time.

"You're not just any ordinary girl, Kritika. You're connected to something much bigger. Your family, your past—everything has been kept from you for a reason."

Kritika felt a sudden chill run through her. **"My family? What are you talking about? What's going on?"**

Neha stepped forward, her voice quiet but urgent. **"You're part of a legacy. A legacy that goes back generations. Your family has been hiding it from you, but I can't hide it anymore. You have powers, Kritika. Powers that have been passed down to you."**

A Legacy of Power

Kritika stared at Neha in disbelief. Powers? She had always felt different, but she had chalked it up to her eccentric love for 90s music, her dreams of a perfect love story, and her unfulfilled longing for something more. But powers? This was something she hadn't even considered.

"Powers? What kind of powers?" Kritika asked, her voice trembling.

Neha's eyes darkened. **"The kind that allow you to see beyond what others can. The kind that help you sense things, connect with people on a deeper level, and even influence events. It's not just about the dreams and the songs, Kritika. You've been hiding it from yourself for so long, but now, it's time to face the truth."**

Kritika's mind was spinning. She had spent so much of her life wondering why she was different, why she had this deep connection to music and art, why she could sense emotions in others even when they tried to hide them. But she had never imagined that it was something more, something inherited.

"Why didn't anyone tell me?" Kritika asked, her voice breaking. **"Why did they hide this from me?"**

Neha's expression softened. **"Your family was trying to protect you. They didn't want you to have to carry the weight of this knowledge. But now, it's too late. You've already been pulled into this world, and there's no going back."**

The Unraveling of the Past

Kritika felt her breath catch in her throat. Everything she had known, everything she had believed, was beginning to unravel before her eyes. **"What do you mean, 'pulled into this world'? What is happening?"**

Neha's face became more serious, her eyes intense. **"There are people who want to control you, Kritika. People who know about your family's legacy and want to use your powers for their own gain. Gagan, for example—he's not who you think he is. He's part of a much bigger plan, one that involves you. He's been manipulating you, testing you. The lies, the betrayal—it was all part of a larger scheme to get you to reveal your true potential."**

Kritika's heart sank. She had trusted Gagan, believed in him when everything else in her life felt like a lie. **"So, everything he said... all of it was a lie? He's been using me?"**

Neha nodded grimly. **"Yes. And he's not the only one. There are others—people you don't know, people who are closer to you than you realize. They're all part of a network that's been watching you."**

Kritika felt the weight of Neha's words settle over her like a heavy cloak. **"I don't know who to trust anymore,"** she murmured.

Neha placed a reassuring hand on Kritika's shoulder. **"You can trust me. I've been trying to protect you, even when it meant keeping secrets. But now, we need to fight back."**

Kritika's eyes flicked to Moni, who had been silent throughout the exchange. **"What about you, Moni? Are you in on this too?"**

Moni hesitated, her expression conflicted. **"I... I didn't know any of this. I didn't realize what was really going on. I've made mistakes, Kritika. But I want to help you now. I'll do whatever it takes to fix this."**

Kritika looked between Neha and Moni, feeling a deep sense of betrayal but also an unfamiliar sense of hope. **"I don't know what's coming next, but I can't do this alone. I need you both. We need to figure this out together."**

The Plan

Neha nodded, her eyes resolute. **"We'll need to go deeper. There are things I've learned—things that could help you unlock your powers. But it won't be easy. We'll have to confront the people who've been pulling the strings**

behind the scenes. And we'll have to do it before they catch on to what we're trying to do."

Kritika swallowed hard, the enormity of the task ahead settling in. **"I'm ready. I don't know what's coming, but I'm ready to face it. Whatever it takes, I'll fight for the truth."**

Moni stepped forward, a newfound determination in her eyes. **"We're with you, Kritika. Let's take them down, one lie at a time."**

Kritika took a deep breath, her mind focused. She didn't know where this journey would take her, but for the first time in a long time, she felt like she was finally stepping into the person she was meant to be.

Chapter 12: The Hidden Society

The Beginning of the Hunt

The days following Neha's revelation were a blur. Kritika couldn't stop thinking about everything she had learned—the hidden legacy, her powers, the mysterious forces that were trying to control her. Her whole life had just been turned upside down, and now, she was plunged into a world of secrecy and danger.

"We need to gather more information," Neha said one afternoon as they sat together in the school's library, away from the prying eyes of their classmates. **"The people who are after you—who are watching your family—they're not ordinary. This is bigger than anything we could have imagined. We need to learn everything we can about the society they belong to."**

Kritika's heart raced. **"A society? You mean like some secret organization?"**

Neha nodded, her expression grave. **"Yes. And it's not just any organization. They've been around for centuries. They've been watching your family's legacy for generations, waiting for the right moment to make their move. And now, it seems like that moment has come."**

Kritika looked at Neha, her mind reeling. **"What do they want from me? What's so special about me?"**

Neha leaned in closer, lowering her voice. **"It's your powers, Kritika. They've been passed down through your**

bloodline. You're not just anyone. You're the key to something much larger than yourself. And they will stop at nothing to control you."

Moni, who had been sitting silently, looked up from her phone, her face serious. **"So, what's the plan? How do we stop them?"**

Neha looked at the two of them, her eyes steely. **"We need to find out who's behind this. We need to track down the people who are pulling the strings. And to do that, we need to get into their world."**

Kritika looked at her friends, feeling a mix of fear and excitement. **"How are we going to do that?"**

Neha smiled faintly. **"We have to infiltrate them. Find a way to get close. Once we're inside, we can figure out their plans. But it's not going to be easy. They'll know if we're onto them. We'll have to be careful."**

The First Clue

The first step in their plan came unexpectedly. During a routine school assembly, Kritika noticed a man sitting in the back of the room. He was dressed sharply in a dark suit, his face concealed by a pair of dark sunglasses. He wasn't a teacher, and he definitely didn't look like a parent or guest.

"Who's that?" Kritika whispered to Neha, trying to keep her voice low.

Neha's gaze followed Kritika's. **"I don't know, but he doesn't look like he belongs here. He's probably one of them."**

Kritika felt a chill run down her spine. **"Do you think he's watching us?"**

Neha nodded. **"It's possible. We'll have to be careful."**

But just as Kritika was about to turn away, she noticed something strange. The man's eyes—despite the sunglasses—seemed to be focused entirely on her. And for a split second, she swore she saw him smile.

The Message

After the assembly, Kritika's phone buzzed in her pocket. She pulled it out to find a message from an unknown number:

"We're watching you. Don't make any moves you'll regret. You can't escape your destiny."

Kritika's breath caught in her throat. **"They're watching me... but how did they know it was me?"** she muttered to herself.

Moni leaned over to look at the screen. **"Who sent that? That's creepy."**

Kritika's mind raced. The message had to be from the same people Neha had warned her about. But who was sending it? And how did they know so much about her?

Neha's voice broke through her thoughts. **"They're getting closer, Kritika. This is just the beginning. We need to move quickly. We can't let them get too comfortable."**

The Secret Meeting

Later that night, Neha called an emergency meeting at her house. Moni, Kritika, and Neha sat around the small dining table, a sense of urgency in the air. The dim light of a single lamp cast shadows on their faces as they leaned in to discuss their next steps.

"We can't stay in the dark anymore," Neha said, her voice steady. **"We need to find out who is behind all of this. We need to get to the core of the society."**

Kritika nodded, her mind buzzing with thoughts. **"But how do we get in? How do we find them?"**

Neha's expression softened, as if she were about to share something she had been keeping from them. **"There's a way,"** she said slowly. **"I've heard rumors about a secret group of people who are involved in this society. They're called 'The Watchers.' They've been keeping an eye on families like yours for generations. If we can find them, they'll lead us to the people behind this."**

Moni raised an eyebrow. **"And how do we find 'The Watchers'? Where do we start looking?"**

Neha hesitated. **"I've heard whispers about a place—an old mansion on the outskirts of the city. It's rumored to be a meeting place for members of the society. But no one who's gone there has ever come back."**

Kritika's heart skipped a beat. **"An old mansion? That sounds dangerous."**

Neha nodded. **"It is. But if we want answers, we have to take the risk. We can't afford to wait any longer."**

A Plan Forms

The three of them spent the rest of the evening planning their next move. They agreed to meet the next day after school and head to the mansion together. There was no turning back now. Kritika knew that she was walking into a dangerous unknown, but something inside her pushed her forward.

As she lay in bed that night, Kritika couldn't stop thinking about the mysterious man in the suit and the cryptic message she had received. She had always felt like there was something more to her life—something beyond the mundane reality she had known. But now, it was becoming clear. Her family's legacy, the powers she had inherited, and the dangerous society lurking in the shadows—all of it was leading her to a place she couldn't escape.

Tomorrow, they would find the mansion. Tomorrow, they would confront the truth.

But what if the truth was more dangerous than anything they could have imagined?

Chapter 13: Into the Shadows

The Journey Begins

The morning sun felt strangely distant as Kritika stood outside her house, glancing nervously at her phone. Neha had texted them both about the plan—tonight, they would meet at the mansion. But Kritika felt the weight of the situation pressing on her chest. She had always dreamed of adventure, but this wasn't the kind of adventure she had in mind.

Her phone buzzed again. It was a text from Moni.

"Ready for tonight? Be careful. I've heard rumors about that place. It's not just creepy—it's dangerous."

Kritika hesitated before replying.

"I'm ready. Let's do this."

Neha's message popped up next:

"Meet at my place at 7:30 p.m. We can't be seen together too much. Stay alert."

Kritika took a deep breath and looked up at the sky. **"I can't back out now,"** she whispered to herself. **"This is my chance to find out the truth."**

The Hidden Mansion

As the evening crept in, a chill ran down Kritika's spine. She and Neha had arrived at the mansion first, standing at the entrance in the growing darkness. The mansion loomed ahead—its tall, weathered silhouette bathed in the dim light of the streetlamp. It looked like something out of a ghost story, its windows like dark eyes staring into the night.

"**This place... it feels wrong,**" Kritika murmured, her voice tight with unease.

Neha nodded, but her expression remained determined. "**We need to go inside. We can't learn anything just by standing here.**"

Just then, Moni arrived, her footsteps echoing through the empty street. "**I've heard stories about this place,**" Moni said, her voice a mixture of caution and excitement. "**People say it's not just abandoned. They say it's haunted by the ones who failed to escape the society.**"

Kritika gulped, glancing at Neha, who didn't seem fazed by the ominous stories. "**We're not here for ghosts. We're here for the truth.**"

The group walked toward the mansion, each of them feeling the weight of the decision. Kritika's heart pounded louder with each step, but her curiosity and the need for answers drove her forward.

Inside the Mansion

The door creaked open with a harsh screech, and the group stepped inside. The air was thick with dust, and the smell of old wood and decay filled their nostrils. The mansion had clearly been abandoned for years, but there was something unsettling about the stillness inside. It felt like the walls were holding their breath, waiting for something to happen.

Neha led the way, her eyes scanning the dimly lit hallway. **"Keep quiet. We don't want to alert anyone if they're watching us."**

Moni pulled out her phone, its dim light casting eerie shadows on the walls. "**This place is huge. How are we supposed to find anything in here?**"

Kritika wasn't sure how, but she had a strange feeling that something important was hidden within the mansion's walls. "**We just need to find something... anything that can point us in the right direction.**"

They moved deeper into the mansion, finding old rooms with cracked windows and furniture covered in thick layers of dust. There were remnants of a once-grand existence—a broken chandelier, a rusted candelabra, a fireplace with faded paintings above it. It was a place frozen in time, and yet it felt alive with the secrets it kept.

As they passed a grand staircase, Kritika's eyes were drawn to a small door at the end of the hallway. It was cracked open just slightly, as though someone had recently passed through. Her instincts told her to go there.

"**What's behind that door?**" Kritika whispered.

Neha followed her gaze and nodded. "**Let's check it out.**"

The Hidden Room

The door creaked open, revealing a room that looked completely different from the rest of the mansion. The floor was pristine, the walls lined with bookshelves filled with dusty tomes. The room had an ancient, almost mystical air about it. But what caught Kritika's attention the most was the large desk in the center of the room, covered in papers and an open book.

Neha stepped forward, cautiously flipping through the papers. "**These are old documents. But they're not just any documents. They're about your family, Kritika. Your bloodline.**"

Kritika's breath caught in her throat. "**What do you mean?**"

Moni bent down to look closer. "**There's a symbol here... It's the same as the one from your pendant. The one your grandmother gave you.**"

Kritika's heart raced. She reached for the pendant around her neck, the symbol that had seemed so ordinary before now taking on a terrifying significance. "**What does this mean?**"

Neha's voice was low, almost a whisper. "**It means you've been marked. This symbol is part of the legacy the society has been watching. They're looking for someone—someone with your powers. And they'll stop at nothing to control you.**"

Kritika's head spun. She had always felt like something about her family was different, but now the truth was crashing into her like a tidal wave. This wasn't just about her future—it was about her entire lineage. And the people after her weren't going to give up without a fight.

Suddenly, they heard a noise from behind them—the sound of footsteps echoing through the hall.

"**We need to go, NOW!**" Neha hissed, grabbing Kritika's arm. "**They've found us!**"

The Chase

The trio sprinted out of the room, racing down the dark hallway as they heard the footsteps growing louder. A dark figure appeared at the top of the stairs, blocking their only way out. It was the man in the suit from the school assembly—the one who had been watching Kritika. He was standing there, eyes locked on her, a sinister smile on his face.

"**You're too late,**" he said coldly. "**This game is over.**"

Kritika's mind raced. She didn't know what to do, how to escape. The walls of the mansion felt like they were closing in on her.

But just as the man moved toward them, a loud crash echoed from the other side of the house. The door slammed open, and a group of strangers burst into the room, all wearing black robes and masks, their faces hidden. They surrounded the man in the suit, pushing him aside.

"**We've been expecting you,**" one of the masked figures said. "**The time has come to bring you to the society.**"

Kritika's heart raced. Who were these people? And what did they want with her?

Neha's voice was sharp. "**We need to run—now!**"

Chapter 14: The Hidden Truth

Escape from the Mansion

The chaos around Kritika seemed to slow down as if time itself was being held hostage. The masked figures stepped forward, their movements synchronized, as though they had been waiting for this moment all along. Their eyes, hidden behind the masks, gleamed with purpose. Kritika's heart pounded in her chest, her breath shallow. She could feel the weight of the situation pressing on her, suffocating her.

Neha, still holding her arm tightly, whispered urgently, "**We need to move, now! This place isn't safe anymore!**"

Kritika, her body frozen in place, turned toward Moni, whose face was pale, her usual confident demeanor replaced by a rare look of fear. "**Moni, what's going on? Who are these people?**"

Moni swallowed hard, her voice barely above a whisper. "**I don't know, Kritika... But they're the ones who have been following you. They know about your family. They know what you can do.**"

Kritika's mind reeled. "**What do you mean? What can I do?**"

But there was no time for answers. The masked figures began moving toward them, each step methodical and slow, as if they were savoring the moment. Kritika's instincts kicked in—she knew they couldn't stay there.

"**We need to find a way out,**" Neha said, her tone resolute. "**Follow me!**"

They sprinted down the hallway, weaving through the darkened rooms of the mansion. The sounds of footsteps grew louder behind them, but Kritika didn't dare look back. Her mind raced, trying to come up with a plan.

As they rounded a corner, they came face to face with the man in the suit again—the one who had blocked their way earlier. His presence sent a chill down Kritika's spine.

"**You really think you can escape?**" he asked, his voice cold and menacing.

Kritika's throat tightened. She was trapped. There was no way out. But just as panic began to rise within her, a sudden noise broke through the tension—a loud crash, followed by the sound of shuffling footsteps. The ground beneath their feet seemed to shake. Something—someone—was breaking through the mansion.

Before anyone could react, the door at the end of the hallway flung open, and a figure stepped through. Tall, cloaked, and exuding an aura of authority, the person's face was hidden in shadow.

"**Step aside,**" the figure commanded in a deep, authoritative voice. "**They belong to me.**"

The man in the suit hesitated for a moment, but then, as if recognizing the figure's power, stepped back. The masked figures around him froze, their eyes widening.

"**Who are you?**" Kritika managed to ask, her voice trembling.

The figure didn't answer right away. Instead, they turned toward the group of masked figures. "**You are no longer needed here. Leave.**"

Reluctantly, the figures stepped back, disappearing into the darkness. The tension in the air eased slightly, but Kritika still felt the weight of the moment.

"**Who are you?**" Neha repeated, her voice firm, though she was visibly shaken.

The figure slowly removed their hood, revealing a face Kritika had never expected to see. It was a face she had seen in her dreams and memories, a face she had seen only once before—a face that belonged to her mother.

Kritika gasped. "**M-Mom?**"

The woman's lips curled into a faint, knowing smile. "**It's time for you to understand the truth, Kritika. Everything you've been told was a lie. And now, you have to decide if you're ready to face the consequences.**"

The Secret Legacy

As the woman—Kritika's mother—led them into another room in the mansion, the atmosphere changed. The air felt charged, thick with anticipation, as though the very walls were alive with hidden knowledge. The room they entered was different from the rest of the mansion. It was dimly lit, with symbols etched into the walls and a large table in the center, covered with old maps and documents.

Kritika stood frozen in the doorway, her mind racing with questions. "**Why didn't you tell me? Why didn't you come back?**"

Her mother's eyes softened, and for the first time, Kritika saw a flicker of sadness behind the strength that had always defined her. "**I had to keep you safe, Kritika. You didn't know the danger you were in. The society... they were watching you, waiting for the right time to make their move.**"

Kritika shook her head, struggling to understand. "**The society? What does that mean? What do they want from me?**"

Her mother gestured to the documents on the table. "**They've been searching for you because of your bloodline. Your father and I, we were part of an ancient order—one that had the power to control the elements. The society seeks to use that power to manipulate the world for their own gain.**"

Moni, still standing quietly by the door, spoke up. "**Is that why you left her? To protect her from them?**"

Kritika's mother nodded. "**Yes. I had to leave, not because I wanted to, but because they were getting closer. They've always known about Kritika's abilities. And now, she's the key to everything.**"

Kritika's mind spun as she processed the information. "**So all the lies... all the things I thought were just dreams... they were real?**"

Her mother sighed deeply, her gaze meeting Kritika's with an intensity that made Kritika feel as though she were looking into the depths of her soul. "**Yes, Kritika. You're more powerful than you know. But you're also in great danger. The society has been preparing for this moment for years. They will stop at nothing to claim your power.**"

The Turning Point

The weight of her mother's words hit Kritika like a tidal wave. She had always felt different, but she never imagined this. The truth was too much to bear all at once, but she couldn't deny the urgency in her mother's voice.

"**What do I do now?**" Kritika whispered, her voice barely audible.

Her mother's eyes flickered with determination. "**You need to learn to control your power, Kritika. You need to prepare for the fight ahead. You cannot let them take what's rightfully yours.**"

Moni stepped forward, her earlier fear replaced with a renewed sense of purpose. "**We're with you, Kritika. Whatever happens, we'll help you.**"

Neha nodded in agreement, her expression hardening. "**We've got your back. We'll fight together.**"

Kritika felt a surge of hope, but it was quickly overshadowed by the realization of what lay ahead. The battle wasn't just for her life—it was for the future. For the truth that had been hidden for so long.

Chapter 15: The Awakening

Training the Unseen Powers

The days following the revelation were a whirlwind of emotions for Kritika. Her mind was still reeling from the truth her mother had shared with her, and every moment seemed to carry the weight of a decision that could change everything. But there was no time for hesitation. The threat of the society loomed over them like a shadow, and her mother was adamant—Kritika had to learn to harness her powers.

In the secluded room deep within the mansion, her mother began her training. The walls, adorned with strange symbols and artifacts, seemed to hum with an energy Kritika couldn't fully understand. Her mother guided her through ancient rituals, some of which felt foreign, while others seemed to resonate deep within her.

"**Focus, Kritika,**" her mother said, her voice calm but firm. "**The power inside you is ancient, but it is also chaotic. If you can control it, you can protect yourself. If not, you will be consumed.**"

Kritika stood in the center of the room, her eyes closed, her arms stretched out before her as her mother instructed. The air around her seemed to shimmer, and a faint pulse of energy began to hum in her chest. It was unlike anything she had ever felt—warm, yet powerful, as though she were connected to the very heartbeat of the earth itself.

"**What do I need to do?**" Kritika asked, her voice steady despite the growing intensity within her.

Her mother's eyes glowed with an intensity that made Kritika's heart race. "**Feel the power. It's inside you, always has been. You have the ability to control the elements—earth, air, fire, water—but it starts with you. Trust yourself, trust the energy within you, and focus.**"

Kritika closed her eyes again, focusing on the sensations swirling around her. She could feel the energy of the earth beneath her, the air that surrounded her, the fire in her veins. Slowly, she let go of the fear that had gripped her heart. The world seemed to fade away, leaving only her connection to this raw, untamed power.

For a moment, she felt nothing—just emptiness. But then, as if in response to her surrender, a surge of energy shot through her. The room seemed to vibrate as the elements responded to her call. A flicker of flame danced at her fingertips, and the wind swirled around her body.

"**Yes,**" her mother said, her voice filled with pride. "**You're doing it. Now, control it. Let it move with your thoughts. Direct it with purpose.**"

Kritika focused harder, willing the flames to rise and then dissipate, willing the wind to form a gentle breeze. With each attempt, the energy became more manageable, but each time she let it go too far, the room would tremble, and her mother would call for her to rein it back in.

"**Balance,**" her mother murmured, "**It's about balance. Control it, or it will control you.**"

Unwanted Visitors

Days passed in a blur of training. Each morning was dedicated to mastering her powers, while each evening brought more questions, more discoveries about her family's past. But Kritika knew there was no time to rest—she had to prepare for the day when the society would come for her.

One evening, after a particularly intense session of training, Kritika stood by the mansion's window, gazing out into the night. The cool breeze kissed her skin, and for the first time in a long while, she felt a sense of calm.

But that calm was shattered when a figure appeared at the gate—distant but unmistakable. She could sense it before she saw it—another presence like her own. It was the society, and they were getting closer.

"**We need to move, now,**" Neha said, bursting into the room, her face pale with urgency.

Moni, following closely behind, looked just as serious. "**They've found us, Kritika. We need to be ready.**"

Kritika's heart raced as she turned to her mother. "**What do we do? Are we ready?**"

Her mother's face was grim. "**They've been watching us for years. We're as ready as we'll ever be, but you have to trust your instincts. You can't let them get the upper hand.**"

Kritika nodded, a newfound determination lighting her eyes. The weight of her family's legacy was heavy, but she wasn't going to let fear dictate her future. "**Let's end this.**"

The First Confrontation

The mansion's perimeter was secured, but Kritika knew it wouldn't hold for long. She had to be ready for the inevitable—an attack from the society. Her mother stood beside her, offering the final piece of advice before the battle began.

"**Remember, Kritika,**" her mother said softly. "**This isn't just about survival. It's about protecting what's sacred. You have a responsibility now, not just to yourself, but to the world.**"

Kritika's heart beat faster, but her resolve only grew stronger. "**I understand.**"

Just as the night seemed to stretch on in a tense silence, the first blow struck. The windows shattered as figures in dark robes stormed into the mansion. They moved with terrifying precision, their eyes cold and merciless. The society had arrived.

"**Stay close,**" her mother commanded, and the three girls huddled together as they prepared to defend their home.

Kritika's mind raced, her heart pounding in her chest as she summoned the power within her. The elements roared to life around her, her hands sparking with electricity, her feet grounded in the earth. She could feel the air pressure shift, the fire building inside her veins, but the fear was there too—this was real, this was happening.

"**You can't escape your destiny, Kritika,**" a voice called out from the shadows. One of the society members, cloaked in black, stepped forward.

Kritika took a deep breath, steeling herself. "**I'm not running anymore.**"

In an instant, the world around her erupted into chaos. Flames shot from her hands, winds whipped through the air, and the ground beneath their feet cracked as she unleashed the power within. But even with all her training, she realized that this battle would not be easy.

The society was strong—too strong for her to face alone.

Chapter 16: The Hidden Truths

A Bitter Revelation

The air crackled with energy as Kritika's powers clashed with the society's forces. She had unleashed everything she had learned so far, but it still wasn't enough. Her body was trembling with exhaustion, and the battle felt like it had no end in sight. The society's members moved with precision, their dark magic clashing with her raw, untamed energy. It was a battle of wills—a test of control, strength, and conviction.

"**You're stronger than I thought, Kritika,**" the cloaked leader of the society sneered, his eyes gleaming with a sinister light. "**But power is nothing without knowledge. And you, my dear, are still so blind.**"

Kritika faltered for a moment, her energy waning. "**What do you mean?**" she demanded, her voice shaky, but fierce.

The leader smirked, taking a step closer to her, his eyes never leaving hers. "**You think you know your true potential, but you haven't even scratched the surface. Your mother has kept you in the dark all these years. You are destined for far greater things than you realize.**"

Her heart skipped a beat. Was her mother hiding something from her? Could there be a deeper truth behind her powers, something that she hadn't been told?

As if reading her thoughts, the leader continued. "**You were born for this. The blood that runs through your veins**

connects you to the ancient ones, to a legacy that goes beyond this world. But your mother—she's been protecting you from the truth, from the truth of your true nature. And now, it's too late to hide it from you."
Kritika's mind raced. The words were too much to absorb, but she could feel something stirring deep inside her. It was as if a part of her had been waiting to hear this, even though she wasn't sure what it meant.

The Power Within

The leader's words echoed in her mind as the battle raged on. Her mother's face appeared in her thoughts, her calm yet distant eyes, the years of secrecy. She had always been protective, shielding her from the outside world, but now, in this moment, Kritika could feel that something had been withheld from her—something important.
"**Your powers are not just a gift, Kritika,**" the leader's voice cut through her thoughts. "**They are a weapon, a key to something far more dangerous. The society wants to control that power. They want to use you as a pawn in a game much bigger than any of us.**"
Kritika shook her head, her mind foggy. "**I don't want any part of your game,**" she spat.
The leader laughed, a cruel, chilling sound. "**You don't have a choice. It's in your blood. You're tied to something that you cannot escape. Your path is already chosen.**"
Her mother had always said there was something special about her. But was this what she had meant? Was it all true?

A wave of exhaustion hit Kritika, and for a brief moment, she faltered. The energy around her began to wane. Her powers were starting to slip through her grasp. The society members closed in, sensing her vulnerability.

Just as they were about to strike, a force of energy surged from within Kritika, more powerful than anything she had ever felt before. The ground beneath her feet cracked open as she raised her hands, sending a surge of light into the air. The society members recoiled, their faces twisted in disbelief.

"**You... you're not just some weak girl,**" the leader whispered, his eyes wide with fear. "**You're... you're the one they feared.**"

The revelation hit her like a wave. Her true potential was far beyond what she had imagined. Her powers weren't just a part of her—she was the key to something ancient, something far more dangerous than the society could ever understand.

The Battle for Truth

The society members began to retreat, their fear evident in their movements. But the leader, still determined, locked eyes with Kritika.

"**This isn't over,**" he hissed, disappearing into the shadows with his followers.

Kritika stood there, panting, her body shaking with the aftereffects of the battle. She felt a rush of emotions—

confusion, fear, but also power, an overwhelming sense of control that she had never known before.

Her mother rushed to her side, her face full of concern. "**Kritika, are you all right?**"

Kritika's eyes were wide with realization. "**What did he mean? What did he mean about my blood, my destiny?**"

Her mother's face darkened. She hesitated for a long moment before speaking, her voice heavy with the weight of secrets long buried.

"**It's time you knew everything, Kritika. It's time to tell you the truth.**"

The words hung in the air like a threat, and Kritika braced herself for whatever her mother was about to reveal. The world around her seemed to hold its breath.

"**You are part of a long lineage of guardians—protectors of the balance between worlds,**" her mother began, her voice barely a whisper. "**Your powers are not just a gift—they are a responsibility. You were born to protect this world, and the worlds beyond it, from the darkness that threatens to consume us all.**"

Kritika's heart raced as she listened, unable to fully comprehend the magnitude of what her mother was saying.

"**But why didn't you tell me before?**" Kritika demanded, her voice trembling with anger and betrayal. "**Why keep me in the dark?**"

Her mother looked at her with deep sadness. "**Because, Kritika, the truth is dangerous. There are forces out there that will stop at nothing to control you, to make you one of them. I've protected you from this world for as long as**

I could, but now, you have to face it. You have to choose your own path."

The Crossroads

The night grew heavy with silence as Kritika absorbed the revelation. Everything she had known about herself, about her life, had just been turned upside down. She wasn't just an ordinary girl. She was a guardian, a protector with powers that could change the fate of the world.

But the society's words echoed in her mind. "**You have no choice.**" Was that true? Was her destiny already written for her?

Her mother's voice broke through her thoughts. "**You must understand, Kritika, this power inside you is both a gift and a curse. You have the ability to change the world, but with that comes great responsibility. The society seeks to control you, but if they succeed, they will use you to unleash forces that could destroy everything we hold dear.**"

Kritika's gaze hardened. She knew what she had to do. She had to take control of her own fate. But how could she fight something as ancient and powerful as the society?

"**What do I do now?**" she asked, her voice firm but filled with uncertainty.

Her mother took her hands, her grip warm and steady. "**You train. You learn to control your powers. But most importantly, you stay true to yourself. The society wants you to become something you're not, Kritika. You must**

resist that temptation. You are more than your powers. You are who you choose to be."

Kritika nodded, feeling the weight of her mother's words. She had a long road ahead of her, and it would not be easy. But one thing was certain—she would no longer let fear control her.

Chapter 17: The Training Begins

The Weight of the World

The next few days were a blur of emotions, conflicting thoughts, and the daunting reality of Kritika's newfound destiny. She had always been a fighter, but this was different. She wasn't just fighting for survival anymore—she was fighting for the very balance of the worlds.

Her mother had taken her to a secluded place, far from prying eyes. A place hidden from the world, where the ancient guardians had once trained. A place where Kritika's powers could be honed, refined, and understood. The air here was thick with history, and every step she took seemed to echo with the whispers of those who had come before her.

"**This is where you'll learn to control your abilities,**" her mother had told her. "**This is where your true training begins.**"

Kritika had a million questions, but none of them seemed to matter as much as the task at hand. She was now a part of something much bigger than herself. The weight of that truth was heavy on her shoulders, but it was also something she couldn't ignore.

As she walked through the dense forest, her senses heightened. She could feel the energy around her, pulsing with life. It was as if the very earth was alive, breathing with her. She closed her eyes and focused, trying to attune herself to the world's natural rhythms. She could feel the ancient magic around her, a force far greater than anything she had encountered before.

The Mentor

Her mother had been her only teacher until now, but it was clear that Kritika would need more guidance if she was to unlock her full potential. That's when they met the mentor—a mysterious figure, a former guardian who had long since left the order, disillusioned with the society and the world they had created.

He was an old man, his hair white as snow and his face lined with the wisdom of many years. His eyes, however, were sharp and piercing, as if they could see straight through her. There was an unsettling calmness about him, as though he knew things that no one else did.

"**You must let go of everything you think you know,**" he said, his voice deep and steady. "**The power inside you is wild, unrefined. It will not be tamed by force alone.**"

Kritika frowned, her fists clenched. She had always believed that power was something to be controlled, something that could be wielded with strength and precision. But this man seemed to be telling her something different.

"**What do you mean?**" she asked, her voice uncertain.

The mentor smiled, his expression one of knowing. "**The power inside you comes from the heart of the earth itself. It is not something you can control with will alone. You must learn to listen, to surrender to the energy that flows through you.**"

Kritika was taken aback. "**Surrender?**"

"**Yes,**" he said simply. "**You must learn to trust the flow of energy, to merge with it. Only then can you truly harness your powers.**"

It was a concept that was difficult for her to grasp. She had always been taught that power was something to be conquered, something to be mastered through sheer will. But here, in this strange place, her mother's mentor was telling her to do the opposite—to surrender, to trust.

The First Lesson

The first lesson was simple, but difficult. The mentor guided her to a small clearing, surrounded by ancient trees whose trunks seemed to hum with energy. He instructed her to close her eyes and focus on the energy around her.

"**Feel the earth beneath you,**" he said. "**Feel the energy that runs through every living thing. Let it enter you, let it fill you.**"

Kritika obeyed, closing her eyes and taking a deep breath. She could feel the energy, faint at first, like a distant hum. Slowly, it grew stronger, like the beat of a drum in the distance, calling to her. The wind rustled through the trees, and she could hear the leaves whispering in a language she couldn't understand.

"**Now, let it flow through you,**" the mentor's voice guided her.

She concentrated, focusing on the pulse of the earth beneath her feet. She imagined the energy rising from the ground, flowing up through her legs, into her core. It was a strange sensation—like being filled with a force that was both foreign and familiar. She felt her body tremble with the intensity of it.

But just as quickly as it had come, the energy seemed to slip away, like water running through her fingers.

"**You're holding on too tightly,**" the mentor said. "**Let go. Trust it to move freely through you.**"

Kritika's brow furrowed in frustration. "**I don't understand. I'm trying!**"

"**You're trying to control it,**" he said gently. "**That's the first mistake. You cannot control what you don't understand. You must learn to surrender, to flow with it.**"

It took hours of practice before she could even feel a semblance of the power flowing freely within her. Each time she tried, it was like trying to catch the wind with her bare hands. But with each attempt, the connection grew stronger, and a sense of calm settled over her.

The Bond with the Earth

Days turned into weeks, and Kritika's training became more intense. The mentor pushed her beyond her limits, forcing her to confront the parts of herself she had always ignored—the fear, the anger, the doubt. Every time she thought she had mastered something, he would challenge her again, forcing her to grow.

She spent hours meditating, focusing on the energy within her, letting it flow through her without resistance. Slowly, she began to feel a bond with the earth itself—a connection that ran deeper than anything she had ever known. She could feel the rhythm of the world, the pulse of life in everything around her.

But it wasn't just the earth's energy she was tapping into. There was something else, something ancient and powerful, running through her veins. She could feel it when she meditated, when she connected with the earth's energy. It was a force that had been hidden from her for so long, waiting for her to discover it.

The Test

One day, the mentor led her to a secluded temple hidden deep in the forest. The air around it was thick with ancient magic, and the very walls seemed to hum with power.

"**This is the final test,**" the mentor said, his voice low and serious. "**Here, you will face your fears. You will confront the darkness that lies within you.**"

Kritika's heart raced. She had been training for this moment, but she didn't know if she was ready.

"**What do I need to do?**" she asked, her voice steady despite the fear that gnawed at her.

"**Trust yourself,**" he replied. "**Trust the power that flows through you.**"

With a deep breath, Kritika stepped into the temple, the air growing colder with every step. Shadows danced on the walls, and she could feel a dark presence watching her. She took a deep breath, focusing on the energy within her.

As she moved deeper into the temple, she felt it—a surge of darkness, a presence that seemed to seep into her very soul.

It whispered to her, calling out her deepest fears, her greatest doubts.

"**You're not strong enough,**" the voice taunted. "**You will never be able to control this power. You are nothing.**"

The darkness surrounded her, closing in on her. Her body trembled, and for a moment, she felt the urge to give up. But then she remembered the words of her mentor—"**Trust yourself.**"

Kritika closed her eyes, taking a deep breath. She let go of her fear, her doubt, and focused on the energy within her. Slowly, she let it rise, drawing on the power of the earth, the magic inside her. It surged through her, a wave of light pushing back the darkness.

With a final burst of energy, she expelled the darkness from the temple, sending it scattering into the shadows. The oppressive feeling lifted, and the temple was filled with a calming light.

A New Beginning

Kritika stood there, breathing heavily, her body trembling with the aftereffects of the test. She had done it. She had faced her fears and conquered them. The darkness no longer held power over her.

The mentor stood behind her, watching silently. "**You have passed the test,**" he said, his voice filled with approval. "**You have learned to trust yourself. But this is just the beginning. The real challenges lie ahead.**"

Kritika nodded, a sense of clarity settling over her. She had come a long way, but her journey was far from over. She had only just begun to understand the true extent of her powers, and she knew that there was still much more to learn.

The path ahead would be difficult, but Kritika was no longer afraid. She was ready to face whatever came next.

Chapter 18: The Gathering Storm

A World on the Brink

Kritika stood at the edge of the forest, her senses alert as the winds whispered through the trees. It had been weeks since her final test in the temple, and although she had gained a deeper understanding of her powers, she still felt the weight of the world pressing on her shoulders. She wasn't just learning to control her energy anymore; she was preparing for something much bigger—something that was beyond her current grasp.

The mentor had warned her that the balance between the realms was fragile. For centuries, the guardians had kept the peace, ensuring that the forces of light and darkness remained in harmony. But now, that balance was in jeopardy. The darkness that Kritika had felt in the temple was just the beginning of a greater evil that was beginning to stir.

Her mother had been silent for days, her usual calm demeanor replaced by a look of concern that Kritika had never seen before. It was as if the very air around them was thick with tension, and the more Kritika learned, the more she realized how dangerous the path ahead would be.

"**The time is near,**" her mother had said earlier that day, her voice low. "**The forces that threaten our world are gathering. They will stop at nothing to plunge it into chaos.**"

Kritika had felt a chill run down her spine. She wasn't sure if it was the weight of her mother's words or the growing sense of dread that hung over them like a storm cloud.

A Call to Arms

The next morning, the mentor arrived at their hidden sanctuary, his face grim. "**It's time,**" he said, his voice carrying an unspoken urgency. "**The darkness has begun to gather. We must prepare.**"

"**Prepare for what?**" Kritika asked, her heart pounding in her chest.

The mentor's gaze hardened, his eyes narrowing. "**There is an ancient enemy, an entity born from the deepest shadows of the world. It is known as the Void, and it seeks to unravel the very fabric of reality. It has been dormant for centuries, but it is awakening now. You are the key to stopping it.**"

Kritika's mind reeled. The Void. The very name of the enemy sent a shiver of fear through her. She had heard stories of the Void, tales passed down through generations, stories that painted it as an unstoppable force of destruction.

"**But how?**" Kritika asked, her voice barely a whisper. "**How can I stop something so powerful?**"

The mentor placed a hand on her shoulder. "**You are not alone in this. You have allies, people who have been preparing for this moment as long as you have. But you must gather them. Together, you can face the darkness, but only if you are united.**"

The First Ally

Kritika had little time to waste. The mentor had given her a name—a powerful sorceress who lived in the far reaches of the northern mountains. It was said that she had the ability to manipulate the elements themselves, bending the forces of nature to her will. Her name was Aria, and she was a legend in the ancient texts.

Kritika knew that she had no choice but to seek out Aria. The Void was growing stronger by the day, and the more allies she could gather, the better their chances would be.

The journey was long and treacherous, but Kritika's determination pushed her forward. She traveled through dense forests, across frozen lakes, and over towering mountains. Along the way, she encountered strange creatures—some helpful, others hostile. Her powers were tested at every turn, but she continued, driven by the knowledge that she was part of something far greater than herself.

The Meeting

After days of travel, Kritika finally arrived at the foot of the northern mountains. The landscape here was harsh—sharp peaks that seemed to pierce the sky and endless stretches of snow. She could feel the elements themselves pushing against her, as if nature itself was testing her resolve.

When she finally reached the peak where Aria was said to reside, she found the sorceress standing atop a cliff, her arms raised to the sky. The wind howled around her, but Aria remained still, her long white hair flowing like a river of silver in the gusts.

"**You have come,**" Aria said without turning, her voice carrying an ancient power.

Kritika stepped forward cautiously, her heart pounding. "**I've come for your help,**" she said. "**The Void is awakening, and I need you to join me in stopping it.**"

Aria turned to face her, her piercing blue eyes glowing with an inner light. "**The Void is not something that can be stopped by force alone,**" she said, her tone grave. "**It is a force that feeds on fear, on doubt. To defeat it, you must first conquer the darkness within yourself.**"

Kritika frowned. "**I've already faced my fears. I've learned to control my powers.**"

"**It is not enough,**" Aria said. "**You must learn to see the world through new eyes, to understand the true nature of balance. Only then can you defeat the Void.**"

The words struck Kritika like a bolt of lightning. She had been so focused on the battle ahead that she had never stopped to truly understand the forces she was up against. She realized that Aria was right—the Void was not just an external enemy. It was a manifestation of everything that existed within her, within all of them. Fear. Doubt. Darkness.

A Lesson in Balance

For the next few weeks, Kritika trained under Aria's guidance. Unlike the mentor, who had focused on honing her powers, Aria taught her to see the world differently. She taught her to read the flow of energy in nature, to understand how every action created a ripple in the universe.

"**You are not separate from the world around you,**" Aria explained one day as they sat beneath the shadow of a great oak tree. "**You are a part of it. Every living thing, every creature, every element, is interconnected. The Void seeks to break that connection. It thrives on division, on dissonance.**"

Kritika listened intently, her mind expanding with each lesson. She realized that defeating the Void wasn't about strength alone. It was about understanding, about embracing the balance between light and darkness, creation and destruction.

The Second Ally

With Aria by her side, Kritika continued her journey to gather allies. The next was a warrior, a protector of the sacred lands known as Kael. His reputation preceded him—he was a master swordsman, a man whose skills were unmatched in battle. However, unlike many warriors, Kael sought peace over violence, using his strength only when absolutely necessary.

Kritika sought him out in a distant village on the edge of the war-torn lands. When she found him, he was training in the village square, his movements fluid and precise as he sparred with other villagers. His presence exuded power, but there was a calmness to him that spoke of inner peace.

"**You seek me for battle,**" Kael said, his voice calm but firm as he wiped the sweat from his brow. "**But I do not fight for glory or conquest. I fight to protect those who cannot protect themselves.**"

Kritika nodded. "**I need you to protect the balance. The Void is coming, and we need your strength.**"

Kael considered her words for a long moment before nodding. "**Then we fight together. But remember, it is not just strength that will win this battle—it is unity, and the will to protect the light.**"

The Path Forward

With Aria and Kael by her side, Kritika now had the beginnings of a team. But there were many more to find—other allies, other powerful beings who had a role to play in the coming war. Time was running out, and the Void's power was growing stronger with every passing day.

Kritika felt the weight of her responsibilities more than ever. The path ahead was uncertain, but she was no longer alone. She had a team of warriors, sorceresses, and protectors by her side. And together, they would face the darkness that threatened to consume their world.

Chapter 19: The Light and the Darkness

The Burden of Destiny

As Kritika, Aria, and Kael continued their journey, the weight of their mission grew heavier. They had traveled through countless lands, gathering allies and facing dangers at every turn. The closer they came to the heart of the Void's awakening, the more intense the energies around them became. There was a pervasive sense of unease, a feeling that they were walking on the edge of an abyss.

Despite the strength of their alliance, doubts lingered in Kritika's heart. Was she truly ready for what was to come? Could she, with her powers still in their infancy, face the darkness that threatened to unravel everything?

"**You carry the burden of this mission alone, but you are never truly alone,**" Aria had said one evening as they sat around a fire, her voice soft but firm. "**The light within you is the key. Do not doubt it.**"

But even as Aria spoke, Kritika could feel the darkness encroaching. There were whispers on the wind, shadows that seemed to follow their every move. The Void was aware of them, and it was patient. It had waited for centuries to awaken. It would not be so easily defeated.

The Secrets of the Void

Kritika's growing concerns were compounded by the mysteries surrounding the Void. No one knew exactly what the Void was, only that it was an ancient evil older than the world itself. Some believed it was the embodiment of all negative energy—fear, hate, jealousy, and rage—while others believed it to be a primordial force of destruction that sought to undo the very fabric of reality.

But what Kritika had learned from the mentor and Aria was that the Void wasn't just an external force. It had a presence within every living being, a darkness that existed in the hearts of people everywhere. To fight the Void was to confront not just the outside threat, but the shadows within.

"**The Void feeds on what you fear most,**" Aria had warned her. "**It will try to lure you into its grasp by showing you the worst parts of yourself. Do not succumb to it.**"

Kritika had always believed that her strength lay in her ability to control her powers, to fight through the obstacles before her. But now, she understood that the true battle was one within herself. If she was to defeat the Void, she had to confront the parts of her soul that she had long kept buried—the doubts, the insecurities, the fears she had ignored for so long.

The Dark Forest

Their journey led them to the Dark Forest, a place known for its malevolent energy and twisted trees. The air here was thick with an oppressive weight, and even the bravest souls hesitated to enter. It was said that the forest itself was alive, that it could read the minds of those who entered and feed on their fears.

As they walked deeper into the forest, Kritika felt the air growing heavier, her every step slow and deliberate. The trees loomed over them like ancient sentinels, their gnarled branches reaching out as if trying to ensnare them.

"**This place,**" Kael said, his voice low, "**It is a reflection of the Void itself. We must tread carefully.**"

Kritika could feel the pull of the darkness here, as if the forest itself was trying to drag her into its depths. She had to stay focused. "**We must continue,**" she said, her voice steady despite the fear that crept up her spine. "**We can't turn back now.**"

But even as she spoke those words, she could feel the darkness calling to her. The shadows in the corners of her vision seemed to grow larger, more tangible. There were whispers now, voices that seemed to echo in her mind, telling her that she was not strong enough, that she would fail, that the Void was already inside her.

The Trial of Shadows

As they ventured deeper, the shadows began to take shape. Figures materialized in the dark, twisted versions of their greatest fears and regrets. Kael's fear was a monster from his past—an enemy he had been unable to defeat. Aria's fear was a vision of herself alone, powerless, unable to protect those she loved. And Kritika… her fear was a vision of herself lost in the Void, consumed by darkness, unable to control her powers.

"**You cannot escape me,**" the vision of herself said, its voice echoing with the cold emptiness of the Void. "**You are already mine.**"

Kritika's heart pounded in her chest as she faced this dark version of herself. "**No,**" she whispered, the words barely escaping her lips. "**I am not yours.**"

The vision laughed, its eyes glowing with the same dark energy that pulsed within the Void. "**You cannot outrun what is within you.**"

For a moment, Kritika faltered. The vision was right, wasn't it? The darkness was inside her, in her fears, in her doubts. Could she truly defeat it if she couldn't even face it within herself?

But then she remembered the lessons she had learned from Aria, from the mentor. "**I am not alone,**" she whispered. "**I carry the light of those who came before me.**"

With those words, the darkness began to recede, its grip loosening. The vision of herself vanished, leaving behind only the cold, empty silence of the forest.

The Heart of the Void

As they reached the heart of the Dark Forest, they discovered the source of the malevolent energy—a dark crystal pulsing with the same energy that had threatened to overwhelm Kritika. It was a manifestation of the Void itself, a conduit that allowed its influence to spread across the world.

"**This is it,**" Aria said, her voice filled with determination. "**Destroy this, and we can stop the Void from fully awakening.**"

Kritika stepped forward, her heart racing. She could feel the pull of the crystal, its dark energy trying to invade her mind. She reached out, her hand trembling as she touched its surface.

But as soon as her fingers made contact, the darkness surged, and Kritika felt her power being drained. The crystal was feeding on her, trying to consume her energy and her will.

"**You cannot defeat me,**" the crystal seemed to whisper, its voice a haunting echo of the Void itself.

Kritika fought to remain steady, focusing on the light within her. "**I will not succumb to you,**" she said, her voice steady and strong.

With all the strength she could muster, Kritika summoned her energy, channeling it through her hand and into the crystal. The dark energy resisted, but Kritika pressed on, calling on the light that burned within her.

And then, with a surge of power, the crystal shattered, its dark energy exploding outward in a blinding flash of light.

The Aftermath

The forest fell silent. The oppressive darkness that had weighed on them for so long began to lift, the trees and the air lightening as the Void's influence receded. The trial was over, but Kritika knew that this was only the beginning.

"**It's not over,**" Aria said, her voice filled with quiet resolve. **"The Void is not defeated. It is only momentarily held at bay. We must prepare for what comes next."**

Kritika nodded, the weight of the future heavy on her shoulders. The battle had only just begun, and there was much more to come. But for the first time, she felt a sense of clarity. She wasn't just fighting the darkness outside; she was fighting the darkness within herself.

And with her allies by her side, she would continue to fight. Together, they would face the Void, and together, they would bring balance to the world.

To Be Continued...

The light may have triumphed over the darkness for now, but the Void is far from defeated. As Kritika's journey continues, she must confront not just the external threat but the darkness within herself. The battle for balance is far from over—stay tuned for the next chapter in this epic tale of courage, unity, and the power of light.

Chapter 20: The Rise of the Void

A Whisper in the Wind

The dawn after their victory in the Dark Forest brought an eerie calm. The air seemed lighter, the forest less oppressive, but Kritika could still feel the faint presence of the Void, as if it were waiting for the right moment to strike. It wasn't gone—not by any means. The darkness had merely retreated, knowing that its time would come again.

The road ahead was uncertain, and Kritika's heart was heavy with the knowledge that the fight was far from over. The Void was more than an external force; it was a reflection of the deepest fears and regrets of all living beings. It would continue to rise, adapt, and evolve. And no matter how many victories they won, the darkness would always seek a way back.

"**The world is not just a battlefield of light and dark,**" the mentor had said before they parted ways. "**It is a place of balance. You cannot destroy the Void; you must learn to coexist with it. Only then will peace be possible.**"

Kritika had taken his words to heart, but the idea of balancing such an ancient evil with the light of hope seemed almost impossible. The Void was relentless. How could she, with her still-developing powers, balance such a force?

As they left the forest behind, Kritika felt both hopeful and fearful. The Void's pull had not yet left her, and she knew that with every step, they were getting closer to the final confrontation.

The Gathering Storm

As they traveled onward, a storm began to brew on the horizon. Dark clouds gathered above them, blocking out the sun and casting the world in a twilight that seemed to pulse with the energy of the Void. The land itself seemed to tremble, as if it too could sense the coming storm.

They reached a small village nestled at the base of a mountain range. It was a quiet place, the people humble and kind. But even here, Kritika could feel the unease in the air. The villagers spoke in hushed tones, their eyes darting nervously toward the skies.

"**The Void's influence grows,**" one villager told them, her voice trembling. "**It has already begun to seep into our hearts. We fear what it might bring.**"

Kritika listened carefully, the weight of their situation pressing down on her. The darkness was not confined to the forests or mountains; it was spreading across the land, infecting the hearts and minds of all it touched. The Void was becoming stronger, and time was running out.

The Inner Struggle

That night, as they sat by the fire, Kritika couldn't shake the feeling that something was wrong. Her powers were growing, yes, but they were also becoming more difficult to control. She had learned how to channel them in battle, to harness the light within her to ward off the darkness. But the more she tapped into that power, the more it seemed to strain her.

"It's getting harder to keep the darkness at bay," she confided in Aria as they watched the flames dance.

Aria's expression softened, but there was an intensity in her eyes that spoke of a deep understanding. **"The Void is clever,"** she said, her voice low and measured. **"It will exploit any weakness, any fear. It knows that your greatest strength is your compassion, your desire to protect those you love. But it will twist that. It will make you doubt yourself, make you question your worth. You must remain strong, Kritika. The light within you is your anchor."**

Kritika nodded, though the weight of Aria's words pressed heavily on her chest. She wanted to believe it, wanted to trust in the light she carried within her. But the darkness was growing stronger with every passing day. How much longer could she resist its pull?

The Trial of the Soul

Their journey led them to a hidden temple high in the mountains, a place said to be sacred to those who sought enlightenment. The temple, however, was not as they had expected. The once-beautiful structure was now in ruins, its walls cracked and weathered. The air was thick with the scent of decay, and the ground was littered with broken statues and shattered relics.

"**This was once a place of peace,**" Kael said, his voice heavy with sadness. "**But now it's a reflection of what happens when the balance is lost.**"

Kritika felt a deep sense of unease as they entered the temple. The air seemed to hum with energy, a strange mixture of light and darkness that made her skin crawl. It was as though the temple itself was a battleground, caught between opposing forces.

"**This is where the true trial will begin,**" Aria said softly. "**This is where you will confront the darkness within yourself.**"

Kritika's heart raced as she stepped deeper into the temple. She had faced the Void in the forest, but this… this felt different. The energy here was suffocating, and she could feel the darkness pressing in on all sides. It was as though the temple was alive, a reflection of her inner turmoil.

"**You must confront your greatest fear,**" the mentor's voice echoed in her mind. "**Only by accepting your darkness can you hope to defeat it.**"

Kritika closed her eyes, trying to steady her breath. She had faced her fears before, but this was different. This wasn't just about confronting an external enemy. This was about facing the parts of herself that she had long buried—the doubts, the insecurities, the guilt she had carried for so long.

The Shadow Within

As she walked deeper into the temple, the shadows seemed to shift around her, taking on a life of their own. Figures appeared before her—shadows from her past, twisted versions of people she loved and trusted. Each figure whispered words of doubt and regret, trying to break her spirit.

"**You are not strong enough,**" one voice whispered. "**You will fail. You always do.**"

Kritika gritted her teeth, pushing forward despite the whispers. But then, the shadows began to change. They took on her own form, showing her the darkest versions of herself—her failures, her fears, the mistakes she had made.

"**You can never outrun your past,**" the shadow of herself said, its voice cold and cruel. "**You are nothing but the sum of your mistakes.**"

Kritika staggered back, her heart pounding. The weight of her past threatened to overwhelm her. But then, she remembered Aria's words: "**The light within you is your anchor.**"

With a deep breath, Kritika stepped forward, reaching out to the shadow. "**I am not defined by my past,**" she said firmly. "**I am defined by who I choose to be in this moment.**"

As she spoke those words, the shadows began to dissipate, the darkness receding. The temple fell silent, the oppressive weight lifting from her shoulders. Kritika had faced her inner darkness—and in doing so, had gained a deeper understanding of herself.

A New Beginning

When Kritika emerged from the temple, she felt changed. The darkness still lingered, but it no longer had the power to consume her. She was no longer afraid of her own shadows. She understood now that the battle was not just about defeating the Void—it was about embracing both the light and the dark within herself and finding the balance that would allow her to rise above it all.

"**You are ready,**" Aria said, her eyes filled with pride. "**The true battle begins now.**"

Kritika nodded, her heart resolute. The Void was not defeated, but she now understood that it was not something to be destroyed. It was something to be faced, to be understood, and to be overcome. The balance between light and dark was the key to defeating it.

With her allies by her side, Kritika stepped forward, ready to face whatever challenges lay ahead. The journey was far from over, but she knew now that she was no longer alone in the fight. Together, they would face the Void, and together, they would bring balance to the world.

To Be Continued...

As Kritika emerges from her trial, a new understanding begins to take shape. The fight against the Void is not just a battle against an external force—it's a battle for the soul of the world. With each step forward, Kritika becomes stronger, but the true test lies ahead. The question is: will she be able to maintain the balance

between light and dark? Stay tuned for the next chapter in this epic journey.

Chapter 21: The Dark Horizon

The Call of the Void

As Kritika continued her journey, she felt the world around her shift. The balance she had sought so desperately to understand was now part of her. Yet, the pull of the Void still lingered, like a whisper in the back of her mind, tempting her to fall back into old fears and doubts.

The land had grown colder since they left the temple. The sun, once a constant companion, was hidden behind thick, rolling clouds. Even the trees seemed to bow in reverence to the shadows that crept across the land. Everywhere they looked, there were signs of the Void's influence—small fissures in the earth, whispers carried on the wind, a heaviness in the air.

"**We must be careful,**" Kael warned, his eyes scanning the horizon. "**The Void is not just a force; it is an intelligence. It watches, it waits. And now that you've faced your inner darkness, Kritika, it will come for you in new ways.**"

Kritika nodded, her hand instinctively reaching for the pendant around her neck. The light that had once felt like a steady flame now flickered, uncertain and faint. It was as though the Void was testing her, pushing her to see how far she would bend before breaking.

The Heart of the Storm

After days of traveling through barren lands and desolate villages, they reached the edge of the realm, where the land met the great Abyss. The Abyss was a place whispered about in legends, a place where the Veil between the worlds was thin and the Void's influence was at its strongest. It was a place where the very fabric of reality seemed to warp and twist.

"**We've arrived,**" Aria said softly. Her eyes, though filled with concern, held an undeniable determination. "**This is where the battle will be fought.**"

Kritika felt the weight of her words settle over her. The Void was not some far-off enemy anymore; it was here, and it was waiting for her.

As they ventured deeper into the Abyss, the atmosphere became increasingly unnatural. The air was thick, almost suffocating, and the ground beneath their feet was slick and unstable. The sky above them pulsed with an eerie violet hue, as if the very heavens were bruised.

"**This is the place where the Void was born,**" Kael said, his voice tinged with both awe and fear. "**Here, it is strongest. If we are to defeat it, we must go to the very heart of its power.**"

A New Ally

Just as they prepared to enter the heart of the Abyss, a figure emerged from the shadows. It was a woman, tall and regal, her hair as black as the night, her eyes glowing with an unnatural light. She was cloaked in dark robes, and her presence felt like an overwhelming force of nature.

"**You seek to destroy the Void,**" the woman said, her voice smooth and commanding. "**But you do not understand it. You cannot destroy what is a part of you.**"

Kritika stepped forward, her eyes narrowed. "**Who are you?**"

The woman smiled, though there was no warmth in it. "**I am Nyx,**" she said, her gaze piercing into Kritika's soul. "**I am the Guardian of the Abyss. And I have been watching you.**"

Kritika felt a shiver run down her spine. "**You've been watching me?**"

Nyx nodded. "**The Void has taken many forms over the ages. It has destroyed, it has consumed. But it also creates. It reshapes, it reforms, and it teaches. You are not its enemy, Kritika. You are its heir.**"

The words struck Kritika like a blow. "**I am not the Void's heir. I fight against it.**"

Nyx's expression softened, though it remained inscrutable. "**The Void is not merely destruction, Kritika. It is creation. It is change. It is evolution. Without it, there is no balance. Without it, there is no life. Do you understand?**"

Kritika felt the weight of her words settle over her. She had fought so long against the Void, seen it only as a dark force that needed to be eradicated. But what if Nyx was right? What if the Void wasn't just an enemy to be destroyed, but a part of something greater, something more intricate than she had ever imagined?

The Truth Unveiled

Nyx led them deeper into the Abyss, into a cavern that shimmered with strange, otherworldly light. At the center of the cavern was a massive crystal, its surface reflecting the void itself, rippling and shifting like a living thing. The air around it was thick with an almost tangible energy.

"**This is the heart of the Void,**" Nyx explained. "**Here, the balance between light and dark is maintained. Without this, the world would fall into chaos.**"

Kritika stepped closer to the crystal, feeling a strange pull. She reached out, her hand brushing against its surface, and in an instant, she was flooded with visions.

She saw herself—her younger self, full of fear, full of uncertainty. She saw the pain she had carried, the guilt of her past mistakes. But then, as the vision shifted, she saw the darkness that had haunted her for so long. It was not an external force, not something that had been forced upon her. It was a part of her, a reflection of her own inner turmoil, her fears, her insecurities.

And then, in a moment of clarity, Kritika understood.

The Void was not something to be feared. It was something to be embraced. It was the reflection of everything that lay beneath the surface of the soul. It was the darkness that allowed the light to shine brighter.

The Choice

As the visions faded, Kritika stood before the crystal, her heart racing. Nyx's words echoed in her mind.

"The Void is not your enemy, Kritika. It is a part of you, and it must be understood, not destroyed."

Kritika turned to face her companions. **"What do I do now?"**

Aria stepped forward, her eyes filled with understanding. **"You must accept it. Accept the darkness within you. Only then can you truly balance the light."**

Kael, too, nodded. **"The Void will always exist. But it does not have to consume you. It can be a source of strength."**

Kritika closed her eyes, breathing deeply. For the first time, she truly understood what it meant to be whole. The Void was not an enemy. It was a part of her, a part of the world. And to defeat it, to bring balance, she needed to accept both the light and the dark within herself.

"I understand," Kritika said softly. **"It's time to stop fighting it."**

Nyx's smile was small but knowing. **"Then you are ready. The true battle begins now, not against the Void, but within yourself."**

And so, with a deep breath and a newfound strength, Kritika prepared to face the final challenge—the battle not against an external force, but against the darkness within. The path ahead was uncertain, but one thing was clear: she would not walk it alone.

To Be Continued...

Kritika's journey has taken an unexpected turn, and the true nature of the Void has been revealed. But will embracing the darkness within her be enough to maintain

the balance, or will it consume her? The final confrontation looms ever closer, and the choices she makes now will determine the fate of the world. Stay tuned for the next chapter in this epic journey.

Chapter 22: Embracing the Shadow

Into the Abyss

With the words of Nyx echoing in her mind, Kritika felt a shift deep within her. The weight of her journey, the battles fought both external and internal, had led her here—to this moment of profound understanding. She was not merely a warrior against the Void; she was its counterpart, its equal. And perhaps, she mused, she had been running from it all along.

Aria and Kael exchanged a glance, sensing the transformation happening within her. They had traveled far and fought many battles, but this one felt different. This was a battle not of swords or magic, but of will, of self.

"**What will you do now?**" Kael asked, his voice filled with quiet anticipation.

Kritika turned toward the heart of the Abyss—the vast, shimmering crystal that pulsed with the essence of the Void. It seemed to call to her now, no longer a threat, but a guide. Her steps were deliberate as she moved toward it, each one heavier than the last, as if the weight of the universe was on her shoulders.

"**I must face it,**" she said, her voice steady despite the storm of emotions swirling within her. "**I must face the darkness within me.**"

The Echoes of the Past

As Kritika stood before the crystal, memories began to surface—memories of her past, of the choices she had made, the mistakes she had carried for so long. The fear of not being enough, the guilt of leaving people behind, the shame of her perceived weaknesses. All these shadows that had plagued her for years now swirled around her, their forms taking shape as they emerged from the depths of her soul.
But this time, instead of fighting them, she welcomed them.
"**You are a part of me,**" Kritika whispered, her voice trembling but filled with resolve. "**I will no longer fear you.**"
The shadows, her fears and insecurities, encircled her, their cold tendrils wrapping around her heart. But instead of suffocating her, they began to melt, their darkness merging with the light that had always lived within her. She understood now that the light and the dark were not opposites—they were two sides of the same coin, both essential for her to be whole.
The crystal before her began to shimmer and pulse more brightly as if in response to her acceptance. The Void was not a force to be feared—it was a force to be understood. It was the space where transformation occurred, where new life could be born.
"**You are the balance,**" Nyx's voice resounded in her mind. "**Without the Void, the light would have no meaning. Without darkness, there can be no growth. Embrace both, and you will transcend.**"

The Test

The ground beneath Kritika's feet began to tremble as the heart of the Void reacted to her transformation. It was not an easy path she walked, and the air grew thick with the tension of the moment. The Abyss seemed to hold its breath as if the entire world waited to see if she would succeed.

Suddenly, the air crackled with energy, and before her, a shadowy figure emerged. It was her—herself, but twisted, distorted, the embodiment of everything she had feared. The darkness she had once fought now stood before her, taunting her, challenging her to face it one final time.

"**You cannot defeat me,**" the shadow snarled, its voice a distorted echo of her own. "**I am you. You are nothing without me.**"

Kritika felt a wave of fear surge through her, but this time, she did not retreat. Instead, she stepped forward, her heart filled with both fear and understanding.

"**I know who you are,**" she said, her voice steady. "**You are my doubts, my guilt, my pain. But you are also my strength. Without you, I would not have come this far.**"

The shadow recoiled, its form shifting and writhing, as if unsure of how to respond to her acceptance. "**You cannot control me,**" it hissed. "**You cannot tame me.**"

Kritika smiled softly. "**I don't need to control you. I just need to accept you. Together, we are whole.**"

The shadow paused, its form flickering, and for a moment, it seemed to hesitate. Then, with a final roar, it merged with her, flowing into her like smoke dissipating into the wind.

She felt the darkness wrap around her, not as an enemy, but as a part of her being.
And with that, the Abyss fell silent.

A New Dawn

The crystal at the heart of the Abyss began to glow brighter, its pulsing light steady and harmonious. Kritika felt a surge of energy, not just from the crystal, but from deep within herself. She was no longer the frightened soul who had first stepped into this journey. She was a being of balance, of light and dark, of creation and destruction. And with this newfound strength, she could see clearly for the first time.
Kael and Aria stood a few paces behind her, watching in awe as she radiated a newfound power. The storm in the air had calmed, and the oppressive weight of the Abyss seemed to lift.
"You did it," Aria said softly. **"You've embraced the Void."**
Kritika nodded, her eyes still fixed on the glowing crystal. **"I didn't defeat it. I became one with it."**
Nyx appeared beside her, her eyes filled with approval. **"You have passed the test, Kritika. You now understand what many cannot: the Void is not a force to be feared, but a force to be understood. A force that is neither good nor evil, but simply is. You are ready."**

The Journey Ahead

Kritika took one last look at the Abyss, now transformed before her eyes. The land that had once been desolate and cold now seemed alive with potential. The Void was not an enemy to be vanquished, but a force that had always existed in balance with light. Now, it was time for her to share this understanding with the world.

"**The journey is not over,**" Kael said, his voice firm. "**You have faced the greatest challenge of all, but there are still battles to be fought. There are still those who will not understand.**"

"**I know,**" Kritika replied, turning toward her companions with a calm determination. "**But I'm no longer afraid. I understand now that I must walk between the light and the dark, and I will do so with strength.**"

The road ahead was uncertain, and the world was still full of challenges, but Kritika knew one thing for certain: she was no longer alone. With her companions by her side and the Void at her back, she was ready for whatever came next.

To Be Continued...

Kritika has embraced her inner darkness and found balance within herself. But the journey is far from over. As she prepares to face the challenges that lie ahead, the world itself seems to shift around her. Will she be able to bring this newfound wisdom to those who need it, or will the shadows once again threaten to consume everything she has worked for? Stay tuned for the next chapter in this epic adventure.

Chapter 23: The Call of the Beyond

Whispers from Afar

The quiet peace Kritika had felt in the Abyss was short-lived. As she, Aria, and Kael made their way back toward the outer edges of the Void, a sudden chill swept through the air. It was as if the very fabric of reality had begun to tremble, the atmosphere thickening with an unseen pressure. The winds carried whispers—fragments of a voice, low and distant, but unmistakably familiar.

"**Kritika...**" the voice called, soft at first, but growing louder, more urgent. "**Come closer, child of the Void.**"

Aria and Kael exchanged uneasy glances, the subtle shift in the air not lost on them. Aria's hand instinctively went to her sword, her senses heightened. "**What is that?**" she asked, her voice barely a whisper.

Kritika turned to her companions, her expression unreadable. "**It's calling me,**" she replied, her voice steady but filled with an unfamiliar unease. She had felt this presence before, long ago, when her journey had only just begun. It was the voice of the one who had first guided her into the world of shadows, the one who had set her on this path. And now, it seemed, they were calling her again.

The wind shifted again, a deep rumble echoing through the ground beneath them. "**Follow me,**" the voice beckoned, now unmistakably clear. "**The time is near, and the balance must be restored.**"

Into the Unknown

Despite the apprehension that gnawed at her, Kritika felt an undeniable pull toward the source of the voice. The darkness that had once seemed so alien now felt like a familiar presence, a companion she could trust. It wasn't just the Void calling her—it was something far beyond, something that existed outside of time and space.

"**We need to be careful,**" Kael said, his eyes scanning the horizon, his sword at the ready. "**This may not be what it seems.**"

Kritika nodded, though she could not shake the sense of inevitability that hung in the air. There was no turning back now. She had made peace with the darkness inside her, but there was something more at play—something far grander than she had yet to comprehend.

As the trio moved forward, the ground beneath them began to shift, the very earth warping as if responding to an ancient force. The sky above darkened, swirling with clouds that seemed to pulse with energy, foretelling the arrival of something monumental.

"**We're close,**" Kritika murmured, her hand reaching out toward the strange energy that crackled in the air. "**I can feel it... Something is about to happen.**"

And then, with a final, blinding flash of light, the world around them seemed to collapse, spiraling into a vortex of light and shadow.

The Realm of the Forgotten

When Kritika regained her bearings, she found herself standing in a place unlike any she had ever seen—a realm suspended between reality and dream. The ground was soft, covered in iridescent stones that shimmered with an otherworldly glow. Strange, translucent trees stretched toward a sky filled with stars that seemed to pulse with their own rhythm, as though the universe itself was alive and breathing.

The air was thick with magic, the scent of ancient power lingering in every corner. It felt as if time had lost its meaning here, as if all things—past, present, and future—were woven together in a delicate web.

And there, standing before her, was the source of the voice. A being cloaked in shadows and light, their form shifting with the ebb and flow of the space around them. Their face was hidden, but their presence was unmistakable—a powerful force, ancient and wise, whose very existence seemed to span the breadth of existence itself.

"**Welcome, Kritika,**" the being said, their voice echoing through the void. "**You have come, as I knew you would.**"

The Truth Revealed

Kritika's heart pounded in her chest, but she stood her ground, unshaken. "**Who are you?**" she demanded, her voice strong. "**What is this place?**"

The being's form flickered, their voice taking on a more ethereal quality. "**I am the Watcher, the keeper of the**

balance. I exist beyond the constraints of your world, in the space between realities. I am the one who guided you, who set the pieces of your path into motion. And now, you have reached the point where the balance must be restored."

Kritika narrowed her eyes, her mind racing to process the words. "**Balance? What do you mean?**"

The Watcher's presence seemed to grow, filling the space with an intensity that made the air shimmer. "**The Void and the Light are not separate forces, Kritika. They are the same. But a great imbalance has been growing, and it is threatening to tear the fabric of your world apart. You have been chosen to bring harmony between them. But to do so, you must face the truth of your own existence.**"

Kritika felt the weight of the Watcher's words settle in her chest. She had always known that there was more to her journey than just defeating the darkness or saving the world. But she had never fully understood the depth of her role.

"**What truth?**" she asked, her voice trembling.

The Watcher extended a hand toward her, and with it, a vision unfolded before Kritika's eyes—scenes from her past, her present, and glimpses of a future yet to be written. She saw herself as a child, fearful and lost, struggling against the shadows within. She saw herself as a young woman, fighting for justice, for purpose. And then, she saw herself now—strong, unyielding, but still carrying the weight of the past.

"**The truth,**" the Watcher said softly, "**is that you are not just a warrior against the Void. You are the embodiment of both Light and Darkness. You are the bridge between them. Your power lies in your ability to accept both halves of yourself.**"

A Choice to Be Made

Kritika stood frozen, the weight of the Watcher's words sinking into her very soul. She was the balance, the key to the forces of the universe. And in that moment, she realized the magnitude of her responsibility. It was not just about defeating enemies or saving the world—it was about reconciling the very essence of creation itself.

"**What must I do?**" she asked, her voice barely a whisper, filled with the weight of everything she had learned.

The Watcher's form began to shift once more, the shadows and light swirling around them in a mesmerizing dance. "**You must decide,**" they said, their voice tinged with both sadness and hope. "**The balance must be restored. The Void has grown too powerful, and the Light has begun to fade. You must choose which force will dominate, or you must find a way to unite them. The choice is yours, Kritika.**"

Kritika's mind raced. She had faced countless challenges before, but this... this was the ultimate test. To choose between Light and Dark, between creation and destruction, between life and death.

But was it really a choice? Could she truly separate them?

"**I will unite them,**" she said, her voice firm and resolute. "**I will restore the balance.**"

The Watcher's form shimmered one last time, their voice carrying the weight of countless millennia. "**Then you have truly come into your power, Kritika. But beware—this journey is not without its costs. The balance must be maintained, but at what price?**"

The Path Ahead

As the Watcher's presence faded, Kritika stood alone, her heart heavy with the realization of what lay before her. She had chosen to unite the forces of Light and Darkness, but the road ahead was uncertain. There would be trials, sacrifices, and challenges that would test every ounce of her being.

"**Are you ready?**" Aria's voice broke through the silence, her hand resting on Kritika's shoulder.

Kritika nodded, her eyes filled with determination. "**Yes. I am ready.**"

And with that, the path forward was clear. The balance had been set in motion. Now, it was time to see where it would lead.

To Be Continued...

✨ Kritika has made a monumental choice—one that will change the fate of the world. But with this choice comes great responsibility, and the forces that govern the universe will not let her go easily. Will she be able to unite

the Light and the Dark, or will the price of balance prove too steep? The journey is far from over.

Chapter 24: The Weight of Choices

The Shifting Path

Kritika's feet felt heavy as she stood on the precipice of the unknown. The weight of the Watcher's words lingered in her mind, a constant reminder of the monumental task before her. As she looked around, she noticed that the landscape was no longer the serene, suspended realm she had entered before. Now, it seemed to be shifting, as if the very fabric of reality was being woven and unwoven with each breath she took.

"**What now?**" Kael asked, his voice breaking the silence that had fallen over the group. He, too, could feel the change in the air, the hum of power resonating around them.

Kritika closed her eyes, focusing on the subtle vibrations that ran through the ground beneath her. The path ahead was unclear, but one thing was certain: she couldn't face it alone. Aria and Kael had stood by her through every trial, every battle. She needed them now more than ever.

"**We move forward,**" she said, her voice steady, despite the turbulence in her heart. "**There's no turning back. The balance must be restored, and it's up to us to find a way.**"

As she spoke, the shadows around them deepened, swirling and coalescing into shapes that seemed to take on a life of their own. From the depths of the darkened ground, eerie whispers rose, like voices from the forgotten corners of existence. The very air seemed to pulse with uncertainty.

The Great Rift

Their journey led them into a vast chasm, a rift between two realms. On one side, the land seemed bathed in light, soft and welcoming, like the calm before dawn. On the other, the darkness was overwhelming, a deep, endless abyss that swallowed everything in its path.

Kritika stood at the edge, gazing into the rift. Her heart raced. She could feel the tug of both realms—the Light calling to her with promises of peace and harmony, the Dark urging her to embrace her true power, to surrender to the primal forces of the universe.

Aria stepped beside her, her expression unreadable. "**Which side do we choose?**" she asked, her voice heavy with the weight of the question.

Kritika closed her eyes, feeling the pull of both forces within her. The answer was not simple, nor was it easy. To choose the Light meant denying the power that had always been a part of her, to turn away from the shadows that had shaped her. But to choose the Dark meant losing the hope that had kept her grounded, the belief that balance could be achieved.

"**Neither,**" Kritika said softly. "**We don't choose between them. We unite them.**"

The Trial of Balance

As if on cue, the rift before them trembled, and a voice echoed from the depths of the darkness.

"**You seek unity?**" the voice asked, its tone both mocking and menacing. "**You are a fool. The Light and Dark cannot coexist. One must fall, and the other must rise.**"

Kritika's heart pounded in her chest, but she stood firm. "**You are wrong,**" she declared, her voice unwavering. "**I am the balance. Both the Light and Dark reside within me. They are not enemies—they are two sides of the same coin.**"

The voice laughed, low and cruel. "**Then prove it. Face the Trial of Balance, and show me that you can truly unite them.**"

Before Kritika could react, the ground beneath her feet cracked open, and she was plunged into a swirling vortex of Light and Dark. The forces collided around her, each trying to pull her in different directions. The light blinded her, while the darkness threatened to swallow her whole.

In that moment, Kritika realized the true nature of the trial. It was not about choosing one over the other—it was about mastering both, about holding onto herself despite the chaos around her.

Mastering the Self

As the swirling forces tried to tear her apart, Kritika centered herself. She closed her eyes, focusing on her breathing, on the rhythm of the universe that flowed through her. She could feel the power of the Light, warm and comforting, filling her with a sense of peace. But she also felt the Dark—cold, fierce, and raw—coursing through her veins, awakening her true strength.

"**I am both,**" she whispered, her voice steady, even as the forces continued to rage around her. "**I am Light and Dark. I am the balance.**"

With a final, resolute breath, she embraced both powers, allowing them to flow through her without resistance. The Light did not overpower the Dark, nor did the Dark consume the Light. Instead, they merged, forming a new energy—one that was neither Light nor Dark, but something more.

The vortex around her began to stabilize, the chaotic forces gradually finding harmony. And in that moment, Kritika knew she had passed the trial—not because she had defeated one side, but because she had learned to wield both.

The Awakening

When the vortex finally settled, Kritika opened her eyes. The world around her had transformed. The rift that had once separated the Light and Dark was now a bridge, a seamless merging of both realms. The land was bathed in a new, vibrant energy, one that shimmered with both the brilliance of the sun and the mystery of the night.

Aria and Kael stood beside her, their expressions a mix of awe and relief.

"**You did it,**" Kael said, his voice filled with wonder. "**You've united them.**"

Kritika smiled, though her heart still carried the weight of the journey ahead. "**The true challenge begins now,**" she replied, her voice steady. "**The balance is restored—but there is still much to be done. We must protect it.**"
As they continued forward, Kritika felt a renewed sense of purpose. She had faced the darkness within herself, embraced both the Light and the Dark, and emerged stronger. But she knew this was only the beginning. The forces of the universe were constantly shifting, and the balance she had restored was fragile. It was up to her to maintain it, to ensure that neither force tipped the scale too far.

The Guardians' Path

As Kritika, Aria, and Kael moved deeper into the heart of the realm, they were met with a group of beings—guardians of the balance. These ancient beings, neither fully of the Light nor of the Dark, had watched over the balance for eons. Their forms were ethereal, shifting between light and shadow, embodying the very concept of equilibrium.
"**You have done well, Kritika,**" one of the guardians spoke, their voice resonating with the wisdom of the ages. "**But the road ahead will not be easy. You must defend the balance against those who would seek to disrupt it.**"
Kritika nodded, her resolve hardening. "**I am ready.**"

To Be Continued...

✨ Kritika has mastered the Trial of Balance, uniting the forces of Light and Dark within herself. But her journey is far from over. As the guardian of balance, she must now protect the fragile equilibrium she has restored. The forces of chaos will not rest, and new trials await.

Chapter 25: The Guardians' Secrets

The Path Forward

The guardians' presence was unlike anything Kritika had experienced before. They were beings of profound energy, radiating an aura that seemed to bridge the realms of Light and Dark. Their ethereal forms shifted with a fluidity that defied the laws of nature. Yet, there was a calmness in their eyes—an ancient wisdom that was both reassuring and daunting.

"**You have passed the Trial of Balance, but the journey is far from over,**" the guardian who spoke earlier continued. "**Now, you must learn the true nature of the balance you seek to protect.**"

Kritika looked around, feeling the weight of their words. The land seemed to breathe with an energy she had never encountered—alive with a harmony that was fragile, yet enduring. She could sense the subtle pull of both realms, the Light and Dark, intertwined in a delicate dance.

"**What must I do now?**" she asked, her voice steady but filled with the anticipation of what was to come.

The guardian raised a hand, and before them, the landscape shifted again, revealing a path that led deeper into the heart of the realm. It was a narrow bridge, suspended over an endless void. A place of transition, neither here nor there, but between realms—a crossing point.

"**This is the Nexus,**" the guardian explained. "**It is the heart of all balance. Here, the threads of Light and Dark**

converge, and it is where the true test of your strength will come. You must protect this place, for if the Nexus falls, so too will the balance of the entire universe."

The Nexus' Secrets

As Kritika, Kael, and Aria approached the Nexus, the air thickened with energy. The bridge seemed to stretch endlessly before them, and the void below pulsed with an otherworldly rhythm. With each step they took, the landscape seemed to shift, as if the very fabric of reality was in flux.

"What exactly is the Nexus?" Aria asked, her voice filled with awe.

The guardian's gaze was faraway, as if seeing beyond the physical realm. **"The Nexus is a place of creation and destruction. It is where the energies of both Light and Dark are forged, where they are kept in balance. It is a place of great power, but also great danger."**

Kael looked at Kritika, his eyes filled with uncertainty. **"And you believe we can protect it?"**

Kritika's gaze remained fixed on the bridge, her thoughts swirling. **"We must. This is the final test of our strength."** She turned to face her companions, the bond they shared growing stronger with each challenge they faced. **"Together, we will protect the Nexus. We will restore balance to the realms."**

The Guardians' Trials

The Nexus was not just a physical place, but a realm of shifting realities. As they stepped onto the bridge, the surroundings began to twist and distort. The world around them seemed to bend, the Light and Dark converging in ways that were both awe-inspiring and terrifying.

Suddenly, a shadow loomed before them—a figure made of pure darkness, its form shifting and writhing. It was not a creature of the Dark, but rather an embodiment of chaos, a manifestation of all the forces that sought to disrupt the balance.

"**You are too late,**" the figure said, its voice like the scraping of metal on stone. "**The balance is already tipped. The Nexus will fall, and with it, the world you know.**"

Kritika's heart pounded in her chest, but she stood firm. "**No. The balance will not fall. Not while I am here.**"

With that, the figure lunged toward them, its form shifting and rippling like a shadow come to life. But Kritika was ready. She reached within herself, feeling the power of both Light and Dark flowing through her. She raised her hands, and the energy of the Nexus responded, illuminating the space around them with a blinding light.

The Battle for Balance

The figure howled as the light surrounded it, but it was not defeated. Instead, it began to absorb the energy, its form growing more monstrous with each passing moment.

"**You cannot defeat me with Light alone!**" the figure screeched. "**Embrace the Dark!**"

Kritika closed her eyes, tapping into the deepest reserves of her power. She felt the Dark swirling within her, raw and untamed. She called upon it, merging it with the Light in a harmonious burst of energy. The two forces collided in a brilliant explosion, and for a moment, the world around them seemed to stop.

When the light faded, the figure was gone. In its place was a swirling vortex, dark and unstable. Kritika could feel the pull of the vortex, threatening to tear the fabric of reality apart.

"**It's not over,**" Aria said, her voice tense. "**The Nexus is still unstable.**"

Kritika nodded, her heart racing. "**We need to stabilize the balance. We need to merge the Light and Dark once again, but this time, we must do it from within the Nexus itself.**"

The Final Convergence

As Kritika stepped toward the center of the Nexus, she could feel the gravity of the situation bearing down on her. The forces of Light and Dark were in turmoil, and only she had the power to restore balance.

"**This is it,**" Kael said, his voice steady but filled with uncertainty. "**The final test.**"

Kritika closed her eyes, focusing inward. She could feel the energy of both realms within her, the Light and Dark fighting for dominance. But she knew what she had to do.

She had to merge them once again, not in a battle, but in a union—a union that would restore harmony to the Nexus and, in turn, to the entire universe.

She breathed deeply, allowing the energies to flow freely through her. The Light and Dark did not fight. They did not clash. Instead, they embraced, weaving together into a singular force—one that was both gentle and fierce, both soothing and powerful.

As she reached out, the energy of the Nexus responded, and the rift that had threatened to consume the balance began to close. The darkness receded, and the light grew steadier, no longer blinding but steady and warm.

The Restoration of Balance

When the energy settled, Kritika opened her eyes. The Nexus was calm, its energies balanced and stable. The forces of Light and Dark had been restored to their rightful place, no longer enemies, but coexisting in harmony.

"**You have done it,**" the guardian said, their voice filled with reverence. "**The Nexus is safe. The balance is restored.**"

Kritika smiled, but there was no time to rest. The journey was far from over. As the guardian spoke, she could feel the subtle vibrations of the universe—shifting, changing. There would always be forces that sought to disrupt the balance, and it was her responsibility to ensure that it remained.

"**The balance is not a one-time victory,**" Kritika said, her voice resolute. "**It is something we must protect every day.**"

And with that, she turned to her companions, knowing that their journey was far from finished. The universe was vast, and there were many more trials to face. But together, they would restore balance, one step at a time.

To Be Continued...

💥 Kritika has successfully stabilized the Nexus and restored the balance between the forces of Light and Dark. But with new challenges on the horizon, she must remain vigilant in her quest to protect the fragile harmony of the universe.

Chapter 26: The Ripple Effect

The Call of the Unseen

The tranquil energy of the Nexus had restored a sense of calm, but Kritika could feel the tension still lingering in the air. The balance was delicate, and though they had temporarily triumphed, the battle for equilibrium was far from over. The weight of the guardian's words echoed in her mind.

"**This is only the beginning, Kritika.**" The voice had been clear—prophetic even. "**There are unseen forces, ancient and powerful, who are watching. The balance you have restored will face new challenges. Be ready.**"

Kritika stood at the center of the Nexus, eyes closed, allowing the energy to flow through her once more. The harmony she had forged with the Light and Dark had created a peace, but the universe was vast, and she felt an unsettling stirring within the cosmic fabric. Something was coming, something she could not yet understand.

"**I need to know more,**" she whispered to herself. "**I need to understand what this truly means.**"

At her side, Aria, who had been silent for a long while, finally spoke. "**Kritika, do you feel that? The pull?**"

Kritika turned to look at her friend. Aria's eyes were wide, her hand resting over her chest as if she, too, could feel the vibration of something powerful and unknown.

"**Yes,**" Kritika said quietly, "**I feel it too. It's as if the balance has awakened something deeper... something ancient.**"

A New Vision

As if responding to their words, the Nexus began to shimmer. A sudden ripple of energy surged through the ground, and the air thickened with anticipation. From the heart of the Nexus, a vision began to form—an ethereal image, fading in and out of focus. It was a map, or rather, a series of interconnected paths that stretched beyond their current realm.

"**What is this?**" Kael asked, stepping closer. "**A vision of the future?**"

Kritika nodded slowly. "**Perhaps. Or a glimpse of what lies ahead. The pathways are not clear, but I can sense... I can feel the presence of a force. A force that is gathering strength.**"

The vision shifted, revealing an ancient citadel perched on the edge of a vast desert. Shadows clung to its walls, and a storm of swirling black clouds encircled it. The very sight of it sent a shiver down Kritika's spine.

"**This place,**" she murmured, "**It feels like the heart of the disturbance. I need to go there.**"

Aria placed a hand on her shoulder, her voice laced with concern. "**Kritika, are you sure? The path you're sensing—it's not a path of light.**"

Kritika turned to face her friend, her expression resolute. "**I know. But I have to. If there is something disrupting the**

balance, I must find it and understand it. I cannot ignore it."

The Journey Beyond

With the vision lingering in her mind, Kritika took the first step forward. The air around the Nexus seemed to part, revealing a pathway leading deeper into the unknown. It was a journey that would take them beyond the safety of the Nexus, beyond what they knew of the realms, into a land where balance was no longer guaranteed.

"**We'll go with you,**" Kael said, his voice unwavering.

Aria nodded in agreement. "**We've faced the darkness together before. Whatever this new force is, we'll face it together.**"

Kritika smiled, grateful for the unshakable support of her companions. Together, they would face whatever lay ahead. The path might be shrouded in uncertainty, but they were ready.

As they walked toward the emerging path, the very air around them seemed to hum with energy. The ground beneath their feet was soft and shifting, as if they were stepping into a space outside of time itself. The realms seemed to blur, and Kritika knew they were entering a domain that was both ancient and powerful—a place where the true test of her strength would unfold.

The Desert Citadel

After days of travel through surreal landscapes, they arrived at the outskirts of the desert. The air was thick with the scent of dust and ancient magic, and the heat of the place felt almost suffocating. In the distance, the citadel emerged from the haze, a towering structure whose walls seemed to pulse with a dark, malevolent energy.

"**This is it,**" Kael said, his voice grim. "**The heart of whatever is disrupting the balance.**"

Kritika's heart raced, her senses alert to every shift in the air. There was a presence here—something ancient, something that had been waiting. As they drew closer, the ground seemed to vibrate, the citadel's dark aura seeping into the surrounding desert like an inescapable shadow.

"**What do you think is inside?**" Aria asked, her voice tinged with a mixture of fear and curiosity.

Kritika frowned, her gaze fixed on the citadel. "**I don't know. But I can feel its power. And it's growing.**"

They entered the citadel, the massive doors creaking open as if they had been waiting for them. Inside, the air was thick with magic, and the walls were adorned with symbols of both Light and Dark—ancient runes that seemed to shift and change as they passed.

At the heart of the citadel, they found a chamber—a vast, circular room with a single pedestal in the center. Resting upon it was a dark crystal, its surface crackling with energy. The very presence of the crystal sent a wave of unease through Kritika, as if it were the source of the disturbance she had felt.

"**What is this?**" Aria whispered, stepping closer.

Kritika stepped forward, her hand hovering just above the crystal. "**This is the source of the imbalance,**" she said softly. "**A crystal that contains the raw energy of both Light and Dark—disconnected, untamed. This must have been what caused the disturbance in the first place.**"

"**Can we destroy it?**" Kael asked, his voice full of urgency.

Kritika shook her head. "**We can't destroy it. But we can heal it. We can merge the energies and restore balance here, just like we did at the Nexus.**"

The Final Convergence

Kritika closed her eyes, focusing on the crystal before her. She reached out with her energy, feeling the chaotic pull of both Light and Dark. This was no ordinary crystal; it was a conduit for immense power, a force that had been left unchecked for far too long.

"**We must unite it,**" she said, her voice calm but filled with determination. "**The Light and Dark must converge here, in the heart of this citadel, just as they did in the Nexus. Only then will balance be restored.**"

Aria and Kael nodded, stepping back to give Kritika space. The air crackled as she summoned the energies within her, merging the raw forces of Light and Dark. The crystal responded, its surface glowing brighter and brighter until the energy was so intense that it threatened to overwhelm them all.

But Kritika held firm. The energy coursed through her, and with a final burst of will, she forced the Light and Dark to merge within the crystal. The dark clouds surrounding the citadel began to dissipate, and the oppressive weight that had hung over the desert for so long began to lift.

Restoring Harmony

The crystal's glow softened, and the room fell silent. The oppressive darkness that had once filled the citadel was gone, replaced by a soft, radiant light that filled the space with warmth. The balance had been restored—not just in the Nexus, but in this ancient place as well.

Kritika let out a breath she hadn't realized she had been holding. The task was not yet complete, but they had taken a crucial step in restoring harmony to the realms.

"**It's done,**" Kritika said, turning to her companions with a tired but relieved smile. "**The balance is restored here, but there is still much more to do.**"

Aria stepped forward, her eyes filled with admiration. "**You've done it again, Kritika. The balance is safe, thanks to you.**"

Kritika nodded, feeling the weight of her responsibility. "**This is just one part of a much larger journey. But we are one step closer to ensuring the balance remains intact.**"

And with that, they turned to leave the citadel, knowing that their path was far from over. The universe was vast, and there would always be new challenges, but Kritika had learned that as long as she had her friends by her side, she could face anything.

To Be Continued...

✨ Kritika has once again restored the balance between Light and Dark, but new forces are at play. The universe is vast, and there are many more challenges ahead. What lies beyond this victory? Only time will tell...

Chapter 27: The Shadows That Linger

A Disturbance in the Flow

The winds of the desert had died down, but something within Kritika's heart continued to stir—an unsettled feeling that refused to fade. Even as the citadel fell silent, the energy of the place lingering in the air, she knew that this victory was only a brief respite. There was a deeper, unseen force at work, one that she had yet to fully comprehend.

As they made their way back through the desert, the horizon before them flickered with strange patterns—ripples in the air that appeared like mirages but felt far more real, more tangible. It was as though the very fabric of reality was trembling.

"**Do you feel that?**" Kael's voice broke through the silence, his tone laced with concern.

Kritika nodded, her senses heightened. "**Yes. The balance has been restored for now, but something is trying to break through. Something darker... more ancient.**"

Aria looked up at the sky, her brow furrowing. "**It's as if the energy we've sealed is pushing back, trying to find another way into the world.**"

"**Exactly.**" Kritika's voice was steady, though the unease gnawed at her. "**It's not over. The disturbance may have been quelled, but the forces we've touched are not so easily contained.**"

They walked on in silence, each lost in their thoughts as the sun dipped lower in the sky, casting long shadows across the barren landscape.

The Whispering Void

By the time they reached the edge of the desert, the air had thickened. The atmosphere was charged, crackling with an energy that felt like a warning. It wasn't the calm, harmonious energy of balance, but rather an eerie, unsettling pulse—like the slow beating of an unseen heart.

As they crossed into the next realm, the temperature dropped sharply. The sky turned a shade of violet, and in the distance, they saw a large archway carved from stone—a gateway to another world, one that seemed shrouded in mystery and foreboding.

"**We're being drawn toward it,**" Kael muttered. "**That archway... it's calling to us.**"

Kritika studied it intently. There was something about the arch that resonated deep within her, a connection she couldn't explain. "**We must go through. Whatever this is, it's tied to the disturbance.**"

Aria hesitated, her hand brushing the hilt of her blade. "**This place feels... wrong. Like a veil between worlds. I'm not sure we're ready for whatever lies beyond.**"

"**But we have no choice,**" Kritika replied, her voice firm. "**The forces we're facing are greater than we can fully understand. We must find their source, and this archway—this passage—might be the key.**"

Without another word, Kritika stepped toward the archway, and one by one, her companions followed.

A New Realm

The moment they stepped through, the world around them shifted. The vibrant desert skies faded, replaced by a dim, twilight-lit world. The air was thick, almost oppressive, and the ground beneath their feet felt unstable, as though the very earth was alive and shifting with the passage of time.

The landscape before them was hauntingly beautiful—dark forests of twisted trees with glowing runes etched into their bark, strange luminous plants that pulsated in rhythm with the ground, and vast plains that stretched endlessly into the horizon, bathed in an eerie, silver light. It was both mesmerizing and terrifying.

"**Where are we?**" Aria whispered, her eyes wide with wonder and fear.

Kritika gazed at the unfamiliar surroundings, sensing a profound energy here, one that felt ancient and untamed. "**This is the Void. Or something akin to it. The place between worlds—the realm of forgotten things. It's a space where boundaries blur and energies converge.**"

"**It's as though the realms themselves are bleeding into one another,**" Kael murmured, his eyes scanning their surroundings. "**This place... it's not natural.**"

As they ventured further into the realm, Kritika could feel the weight of the Void pressing in on her. The air was thick with the remnants of broken promises, lost souls, and forgotten histories. It was a place that thrived on the absence of balance—a reflection of all that had been left unresolved.

The Forgotten Watchers

Deep within the Void, they stumbled upon a clearing—a vast, circular space surrounded by towering stones inscribed with strange symbols. At the center of the clearing stood a figure, cloaked in shadow, its form indistinct but powerful.

"**Who are you?**" Kritika called out, her voice steady despite the overwhelming energy of the place.

The figure didn't answer immediately. Instead, it stepped forward, and as it did, the air seemed to shimmer and warp around it. The figure's shape became clearer—an ancient being, its face hidden beneath a hood, its eyes glowing with an unsettling, otherworldly light.

"**You are the ones who have disturbed the balance,**" the figure's voice echoed, hollow and reverberating in the air. It was both familiar and alien, as though it had existed for eons beyond time.

Kritika stood her ground, her heart pounding. "**We've come to restore the balance, not to disrupt it.**"

The figure laughed, a low, resonant sound that vibrated through the very fabric of the Void. "**Restore? You think you can restore what has been shattered for eons? You think you can control the forces of Light and Dark that have always existed in chaos? The balance is a lie. It was never meant to be. You are merely playing your part in a game that is far older than you can imagine.**"

Kritika's eyes narrowed. "**Then tell me—what is the truth?**"

The figure stepped closer, its presence growing stronger, more imposing. "**The truth is that the Void has always existed—an eternal space where the energies of creation and destruction merge. What you call Light and Dark are but fragments of a greater whole. The true power lies in the Void. You cannot control it. You can only endure it.**"

"**I refuse to accept that,**" Kritika said, her voice steady despite the growing pressure around her. "**I believe balance can exist, that Light and Dark can coexist in harmony.**"

The figure tilted its head, as if amused by her defiance. "**You will soon learn that the Void is inevitable. It will consume all in time, and you will either bow to its power or be lost within it.**"

Before Kritika could respond, the figure raised its hands, and the clearing around them began to distort. The symbols on the stones glowed brighter, and the ground beneath them began to crack open, revealing a swirling abyss.

"**We will see how long your balance lasts,**" the figure intoned, its voice fading as the abyss began to swallow everything around them.

The Abyss Awaits

As the ground cracked and the Void threatened to engulf them, Kritika's heart raced. She knew the stakes were higher than ever, that this was no mere test of strength. This was a confrontation with the very essence of creation and destruction itself.

"**We cannot let this place swallow us,**" Kael shouted over the roar of the expanding abyss. "**We need to close it, to find a way to stop the Void from consuming everything!**"

Kritika's mind raced. The path ahead was unclear, but one thing was certain—this would be the greatest test of her power, of her ability to unite the Light and Dark within her. She could feel it—something deep within her, a strength she hadn't fully tapped into yet. The Void may be ancient, but she was determined to rewrite the ending of this story.

"**We fight together,**" she said, her voice filled with conviction. "**We will not let the Void consume us. We will create our own path.**"

And with that, the battle for the fate of the realms began. The Void was not an enemy to be defeated with force alone—it was a challenge of the heart, a test of will. The Light, the Dark, the Nexus—they would all converge here, in this moment, and Kritika would stand at the center of it.

To Be Continued...

✵ The Void has spoken, and Kritika faces its power. With the fate of all realms hanging in the balance, she must summon the strength to face an ancient force that seeks to unravel everything. Will the Light and Dark be enough to survive the storm?

Chapter 28: Convergence of Fates

The Heart of the Void

Kritika stood at the edge of the abyss, the swirling darkness before her alive with a sentient energy that seemed to pull at her soul. The very air crackled with power, and as she looked into the black expanse, it felt as if it was gazing back at her—watching, waiting, judging.

Her breath was shallow, but her mind was clear. The Void wanted to consume everything, to erase the delicate balance of the realms. Yet, in its depth, she felt a strange pull—a call not just from the darkness, but from the Light as well. They were two sides of the same force, and for the first time, she understood that they were not enemies but necessary opposites, partners in an endless dance.

"**Kritika, we have to do something!**" Kael's voice snapped her from her thoughts. His face was pale, his eyes wide with the fear of being consumed by the abyss. Behind him, Aria stood firm, her hands gripping her sword, though the fear was evident in her stance.

Kritika glanced at her companions. They were scared, yes, but there was also something else—an unwavering resolve in their eyes. She wasn't alone in this. Together, they could face this, together they could stop the Void from spreading any further.

"**We need to reconnect the flow,**" Kritika said, her voice steady but urgent. "**The balance is the key. We can't fight**

the Void with force, but we can guide its power. We can redirect it, keep it contained."

"**And how do we do that?**" Aria asked, her voice strained but determined.

Kritika closed her eyes, drawing a deep breath. She reached out with her senses, feeling the pulse of energy around her. The Void was vast, but it was not without structure. Deep within its center, there was a core—an ancient focal point that acted as its heart. If they could control it, they could disrupt the flow of energy, contain the abyss before it consumed everything.

"**We need to create a conduit,**" she murmured. "**Something to channel the Void's energy into a new form. It's not enough to simply seal it away. We must transform it.**"

Kael furrowed his brow. "**Transform it? Into what?**"

Kritika turned to face them, her eyes resolute. "**Into something that can restore the balance. The Void is not inherently evil—it's simply... forgotten. It represents everything that has been lost or abandoned. If we can merge its power with the Light, if we can use it to heal what's been broken...**"

She trailed off, her mind racing with possibilities. There was so much she didn't yet understand, so much she needed to learn, but one thing was clear: they had to take this risk. The Void would not yield to them easily, but she could not allow it to consume everything.

The Ritual of Convergence

They formed a circle around the abyss, each of them standing tall, their spirits unified in purpose. The energy of the Void was overwhelming, a dark tide that sought to pull them under, but Kritika focused on the light within her. The Nexus of Light and Dark, the center of her power, was the key to bridging the realms.

"**Focus,**" she said, her voice calm but intense. "**Feel the energy between us. This is not just about control—it's about balance. Trust in what we are about to do.**"

Kael and Aria nodded, their hands raised in unison. As their palms turned upward, a soft light began to glow around them, a warm, golden aura. Kritika reached out to them, feeling the connection form. The energy between them grew stronger, their wills intertwined as they channeled their collective power toward the heart of the Void.

The darkness before them quivered, reacting to the surge of light. It wasn't a force of resistance; it was an invitation. The Void was ancient, but it was not invincible. Its power was a tool, one that could be shaped, just as the Light could be.

"**Now,**" Kritika whispered, her voice barely audible over the roar of the abyss. "**Merge the energies. Let the light flow through the darkness and reshape it.**"

The moment the words left her lips, the world around them seemed to shudder. The abyss rippled violently, but instead of consuming everything, it began to twist and bend. The light from the circle swirled into the Void, wrapping around it like tendrils of energy. Kritika felt it—a pull deep within her, a connection between the realms, between all the things she had learned and all she had yet to understand.

Her heart raced as she focused, guiding the flow. The Void responded to her touch, its chaotic energy shifting into something else—a new form, one that no longer sought to devour but to heal. She could feel it—a balance being restored, one that neither Light nor Dark could achieve alone.

"**It's working,**" Kael gasped, his voice filled with awe.

"**Keep going,**" Kritika urged. "**We're almost there.**"

The transformation was gradual, but the change was undeniable. The dark energy began to shift, its violent force turning into something more serene. It was as if the Void itself was being reborn, its destructive potential tempered by the Light.

The Awakening

As the last of the energy was absorbed into the heart of the Void, the world around them fell into stillness. The swirling darkness had receded, leaving behind a strange calmness in the air. The stones around them, once glowing with ancient symbols, now pulsed gently with a soft, silver light.

Kritika opened her eyes, breathing heavily. Her body ached, her senses were overloaded, but she could feel it—the balance had been restored. The Void, once a force of destruction, had been transformed into a source of power for renewal. It was no longer a dark abyss but a place where creation and destruction could coexist, where the energies of the world could flow freely.

"**It's over,**" Aria said quietly, her voice filled with disbelief.

Kritika looked around at her companions. "**It's not over. It's only just begun.**"

"**What do you mean?**" Kael asked, his brow furrowing.

"**This is just one step,**" Kritika explained. "**We've stabilized the Void, but there are other forces at work—other realms that are still out of balance. We've won this battle, but there are more challenges ahead. The true test is yet to come.**"

She turned to face the newly transformed realm, its once-threatening energy now a calm, nurturing force. "**We must continue to learn, to grow, and to protect the balance. Only then can we ensure that this power remains in harmony with the world.**"

The shadows of the Void had been transformed, but the journey was far from over. There were more realms to explore, more challenges to face, and more secrets to uncover. And Kritika, with her newfound understanding of Light and Dark, was ready for whatever came next.

To Be Continued...

✵ **The battle for the Void has been won, but the path ahead remains uncertain. Kritika and her companions now face a new realm of possibility, where the lines between creation and destruction blur. What new trials await them as they venture deeper into the unknown?**

Chapter 29: The Final Convergence

The Path to Understanding

Kritika stood before the heart of the transformed Void, the once chaotic energy now calm and steady like the ocean after a storm. She could feel its pulse beneath her fingertips, a reminder of the delicate balance they had achieved. But there was something still hanging in the air, a sense that they hadn't truly won—not yet, at least.

"**The balance we've created is fragile,**" she whispered, more to herself than to the others. "**We've brought order to chaos, but there's still much we don't understand. The realms are shifting, Kael. Aria. This is just the beginning.**"

Kael stepped forward, placing a hand on her shoulder. "**You've done it, Kritika. You've made the impossible possible. The Void is no longer a threat. We've turned darkness into something we can control.**"

"**Control,**" Kritika murmured, shaking her head. "**Control is an illusion. We need to stay vigilant. The Void might be tamed, but the world around us is shifting. There are other forces at play, and we have yet to see the full picture.**"

Aria joined them, her gaze distant. "**What do you mean by 'other forces'?**"

Kritika turned to her, her eyes burning with determination. "**The realms are not isolated, Aria. They are interconnected. If we've altered the Void, we've set off a chain reaction in other dimensions. We may have balanced one force, but we might have triggered another imbalance.**

We need to find the source of that disruption before it's too late."

"Then let's go," Kael said with a resolute nod. **"We won't let this power slip out of control again."**

Together, the trio stood in silence, contemplating the weight of what lay ahead. They had faced the Void, confronted the darkness, and turned it into a source of potential. But now, they had to venture deeper into the mysteries of the universe, facing new challenges and unknown enemies.

The Gathering Storm

Kritika felt the tremor in the air before she saw it—the subtle shift in the fabric of the realms. The energy around them hummed with an unfamiliar resonance. It was a sound like the distant rumble of thunder, a storm brewing on the horizon. The balance they had created was beginning to crack, and it was no longer just the Void that they had to fear.

"It's happening," Kritika whispered. **"The other realms are reacting."**

She closed her eyes, her senses stretching out across the realms. She could feel it now—an energy unlike anything she had ever encountered. It was ancient, yet powerful, and it was moving through the realms like a tide. She reached out for it, trying to understand its source.

"It's not just a force," she said, her voice trembling. **"It's a being. A consciousness. Something ancient, something that has been sleeping for eons. It's awakening."**

The others exchanged glances, a growing sense of urgency filling the air. They knew what this meant. There was a greater force at work—a force that sought not just to disrupt the balance, but to control it.

The Ancient One

As the group ventured deeper into the unknown, the fabric of reality around them seemed to shift. The path they walked on twisted, as if the universe itself were trying to guide them. The deeper they went, the stronger the pull of the unknown entity became.

Finally, they reached the source—a massive gate that stood before them, its surface covered in ancient symbols that pulsed with power. It was a gateway to a realm that none of them had ever seen, a realm untouched by time.

"This is it," Kael said, his voice low. **"The source of the disturbance. But what is it?"**

Kritika stepped forward, her hand resting lightly on the gate. As soon as her touch made contact, the symbols flared to life, glowing brightly. The gate began to creak and groan, as if something powerful was awakening from within.

"It's the Ancient One," Kritika whispered, her eyes wide with realization. **"The consciousness that governs the balance of the realms. It's been dormant, but now it's awakening. It wants to reclaim control of the Void."**

"But why now?" Aria asked, her voice filled with disbelief. **"Why after all this time?"**

"The Void's transformation disrupted the delicate equilibrium," Kritika explained. "**By altering the Void's nature, we've triggered the awakening of an ancient force that seeks to restore its dominance over the realms. We didn't just stop the Void's expansion; we've inadvertently woken the force that created it.**"

The gate shuddered, and with a resounding boom, it opened, revealing a vast, shadowed landscape. Within it stood a towering figure—an entity cloaked in darkness, its form both humanoid and otherworldly. It was the Ancient One, a being of pure cosmic energy, the embodiment of the balance between Light and Dark.

"**You dare defy me?**" the voice of the Ancient One boomed, echoing across the realms. "**You have tampered with the very fabric of existence. For that, you will pay the price.**"

Kritika stepped forward, her resolve unwavering. "**We did not defy you. We restored the balance that you yourself created. We only sought to heal what was broken.**"

The Ancient One's eyes glowed with an eerie, otherworldly light. "**You cannot understand the forces you are meddling with. The Void is mine to control, and so too are the realms. You cannot keep what you have stolen.**"

The Final Battle

The air crackled with power as the Ancient One extended its hand, sending a wave of energy that sent the trio stumbling backward. Kael raised his sword, but the energy was too overwhelming, too intense for even their combined strength.

"**Kritika, we have to do something!**" Aria shouted, struggling to keep her footing.

Kritika's mind raced. The Ancient One was too powerful, too ancient, to be fought head-on. But there was one thing that could stop it—one thing that could shift the balance once more. She had to go beyond the boundaries of the known, beyond the limits of her own power.

She closed her eyes, reaching deep within herself, reaching for the Light and the Dark, the Void and the Heart of Creation. She called upon the ancient knowledge she had uncovered, the wisdom of the realms, the strength of the collective will of all beings.

"**I will not let you destroy this balance,**" she said, her voice resonating with the power of the universe itself. "**I will become the bridge between worlds. I will not let Light and Dark clash in endless war. I will restore the true balance.**"

The power surged through her, her body alight with an energy beyond comprehension. She was no longer just a conduit; she had become the embodiment of the balance itself. The Void, the Light, the Dark—all of it flowed through her.

The Ancient One recoiled, its power faltering before the raw force of Kritika's will. "**You... you cannot be!**" it gasped, its voice filled with fear.

But it was too late. The energy from Kritika's body collided with the Ancient One's, enveloping it in a swirling maelstrom of Light and Dark. The force of it was unimaginable, a clash of cosmic powers that shook the very foundation of the realms.

With a final cry, the Ancient One collapsed, its form unraveling into nothingness. The gate closed, and the realms fell into an uneasy silence.

Epilogue: The Rebirth

The battle was over. The Ancient One was no more. But Kritika knew this was not the end. It was only a new beginning.

The balance had been restored, but it had come at a cost. The realms were now linked in ways that had never been seen before, and Kritika was no longer just a part of the world—she was its guardian. The Light, the Dark, the Void—they all lived within her now.

As she stood on the threshold of the Void's heart, Kael and Aria beside her, Kritika smiled. The journey had been long, and the challenges had been many, but they had succeeded. The universe was no longer a place of endless conflict—it was a place of balance, where Light and Dark could coexist, where creation and destruction could flow in harmony.

"**We've done it,**" Kael said, his voice filled with awe.

"**Yes,**" Kritika said softly, her eyes shining with the knowledge of all she had learned. "**We've done it together.**"

And with that, they turned, walking away from the heart of the Void, toward the next chapter of their journey.

✨ The End... for now.

Character Arcs

Kritika – The Seeker of Balance

- Starts as an intuitive but uncertain individual, feeling drawn to the mysteries of the Void.
- Through trials, she uncovers her true nature as a bridge between Light and Dark.
- Overcomes doubt and embraces her role as the guardian of balance.

Kael – The Warrior with a Past

- Begins as a protector, bound by duty but haunted by past failures.
- Learns that strength is not just about fighting but about trust and vulnerability.
- Becomes a pillar of support for Kritika, understanding his purpose beyond battle.

Aria – The Scholar Turned Rebel

- A brilliant mind who once believed in order and rules.
- Her faith in the old ways is shattered when she sees the corruption within the Council.
- Evolves into a leader who champions change, forging a new path for knowledge.

The Ancient One – The Awakening Force

- A being that has maintained balance for eons but has grown rigid in its ways.
- Sees Kritika's actions as a disruption but ultimately realizes the need for evolution.

- Fades into the universe, leaving behind a new form of harmony.

Themes & Messages

1. Balance Over Power

- The story emphasizes that true strength lies not in dominance but in balance.
- Both Light and Dark have a purpose; neither should be destroyed, only understood.

2. Transformation and Growth

- Each character undergoes a journey of self-discovery, proving that change is not only possible but necessary.

3. The Power of Choice

- Fate may guide, but free will determines the outcome. Kritika's choices shape the destiny of the realms.

4. Knowledge vs. Wisdom

- Learning facts is not enough; understanding and applying them with wisdom is what creates true change.

5. Unity Across Differences

- The story highlights how different forces—magic and science, order and chaos, past and future—must come together.

Glossary of Terms & Lore

The Void

A mysterious force that exists between realms, once chaotic but now transformed into a source of balance.

The Council of Realms

An ancient order that has long controlled the flow of knowledge and power across dimensions.

The Ancient One

A cosmic entity responsible for maintaining the equilibrium of existence.

The Prophecy of Convergence

A legend that foretells the merging of Light and Dark through a chosen being.

The Twin Moons War

A pivotal conflict that set the stage for the events of the book.

Author's Note

This book has been an exploration of the delicate balance that exists in all things—within ourselves, within the universe, and within the stories we tell.

If you've made it to this page, I hope this journey has sparked something within you: a question, a revelation, or simply a new way of seeing the world.

Thank you for being part of this adventure.

Until we meet again in the realms of imagination,
Raven Dee

www.ingramcontent.com/pod-product-compliance
Ingram Content Group UK Ltd.
Pitfield, Milton Keynes, MK11 3LW, UK
UKHW021407190726
13845UKWH00028B/924

9 789334 232424